Prepare To Die. . .

Two people were coming through the cornfield. Their footsteps were out of sync, and the second intruder was walking several paces behind the first.

I sank back in the shadows, took out Wilhelmina and waited for the two to enter the barn. I wanted to take them alive, but since there were two of them, how could I? Or, for that matter, keep myself alive . . .

NICK CARTER IS IT!

"Nick Carter out-Bonds James Bond."
—*Buffalo Evening News*

"Nick Carter is America's #1 espionage agent."
—*Variety*

"Nick Carter is razor-sharp suspense."
—*King Features*

"Nick Carter is extraordinarily big."
—*Bestsellers*

"Nick Carter has attracted an army of addicted readers . . . the books are fast, have plenty of action and just the right degree of sex . . . Nick Carter is the American James Bond, suave, sophisticated, a killer with both the ladies and the enemy."
—*The New York Times*

FROM THE NICK CARTER
KILLMASTER SERIES

A Killmaster Spy Chiller

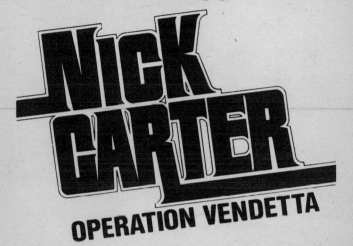

NICK CARTER

OPERATION VENDETTA

CHARTER BOOKS, NEW YORK

OPERATION VENDETTA

A Charter Book/published by arrangement with
The Condé Nast Publications, Inc.

PRINTING HISTORY
Charter edition/June 1983

ISBN: 0-441-63430-3

Charter Books are published by Charter Communications, Inc.
200 Madison Avenue, New York, N.Y. 10016
PRINTED IN THE UNITED STATES OF AMERICA

ONE

Weariness rolled over me like the wheel of a massive earth-moving machine. Wounds and bruises from that harrowing ordeal in Cyprus were like pinpricks of fire over my entire body. Along with the exhaustion, the pain and the lack of proper sleep or medical attention was a hunger as biting as a bee sting.

In spite of it all, I stumbled from the shower in my N Street safehouse, dried halfheartedly and tumbled into bed. In a matter of seconds, I was sound asleep.

Nightmares came.

Greasy Greek guerrillas came at me from all sides, firing a variety of weapons, tossing homemade Molotov cocktails. I was running down an endlessly long pier into the Aegean Sea. Bombs began to fall, along with artillery shells. Great hunks of the pier began to explode in fiery, debris-ridden balls in front and in back of me.

And then I was in North Africa, struggling through hip-deep sand on the Moroccan desert. Planes circled above, dropping firebombs and chattering their .50 caliber machine guns. Copper-sheathed bullets kicked sand in my face and eyes. A bullet ricocheted from a boulder and laced my hips, slowing my escape through the sand, building pain to crescendos achieved only by immense orchestras.

As my hurt and wounded body was being pulled through the dark waters of the Mediterranean toward a distant submerged submarine, I felt something firm and tight on my shoulder. A grip. Someone had me by the shoulder, my wounded shoulder, and was shaking it.

"Carter!" a gruff voice rumbled through the dream. The shaking of my already painful shoulder was becoming violent.

"Oh Christ," I mumbled in my sleep, "can't you let a guy get a minute's rest?"

The bed was suddenly rising in the air, tilting to the left. I felt my body rolling.

"What the hell—"

The grip returned to my shoulder. I smelled garlic, and opened my eyes. Above me, only inches from my face, was the large, round head of a very angry and evil-looking man in a cheap fedora.

"Nick Carter," the gruff voice came from the man's thick lips. "Get dressed. You're coming with us."

Us?

I shook sleep from my mind and glanced around the man with the garlic breath; two other men in cheap hats stood across the room. They held handguns that I recognized as Russian-made copies of a .45 caliber Colt automatic. Beyond them, at the door, was still another man, hatless and with straw blond hair, with his hands in his jacket pockets. His expression was the most sinister.

"Who are you guys?" I demanded. "What do you want?"

"Your name is Nick Carter?" said the man who had me in his clutches.

"I don't know anyone by that name," I said, stalling. I needed a few minutes to get my bearings.

The man maintained his strong grip on my shoulder. I'd taken a big splinter of a Cyprus pier in that shoulder and the wound was too fresh for such pressure. But the man obviously wasn't going to let up until he got a straight answer.

"My name is Raymond Parson," I said, suddenly remembering the name I'd put on the lease.

"You are Nick Carter," the man said in a wave of nauseating garlic. "Get dressed, you're coming with us."

"Look, I don't know who or what—"

The hand squeezed so tightly on the fresh wound that I could only cry out in pain. Tears beaded in my eyes and I felt an enormous pounding in my head. The man saw the pain, grinned swiftly and released his grip.

"Up, Carter!"

The man backed off and I rose slowly. I surveyed the overturned bed and rumpled covers. The man made a head motion to the two men with guns. They pocketed their Colt imitations and went to work setting the place right. I stumbled to the closet, my shoulder throbbing, and began dressing. I turned to the four men, particularly the ugly one who had set my shoulder on fire.

"Just as a favor," I said gently, smiling, "why don't you tell me who you are and what this is all about?"

I had already detected somewhat of an accent—Russian. More a particular part of Russia . . . the Caucasus. Christ, the guy was one step removed from a Mongolian.

"You will be knowing in time," he told me. "No more questioning."

With another motion of his head, he set the two goons to work searching the apartment. The fourth man remained at the door, hands in pockets. The same expertise that had set the rumpled bed to rights was put to use ripping the rest of the apartment to shreds. I didn't worry about the search. I called this my "safehouse" because it contained none of my special weapons—not Wilhelmina, my Luger; not Hugo, my stiletto; and not Pierre, my gas bomb.

One of the searchers came out of the closet with a briefcase and brought it to the big ugly man. On it were the initials, in gold, RP.

"Your case?"

I nodded. The movement hurt, so I mumbled a quiet, "Yes, it's mine."

"The key, please."

I had been weary when I'd arrived, but not too weary to set up a backdrop. I took my jacket from the closet, started to reach into the left pocket, and the ugly man snatched it from me. The man found the briefcase key and opened it. He spread the contents on the newly made bed.

After studying the contents for a very long time, as I continued to dress and get my nerves back in place, the man turned to me.

"According to this bunch of lies," he said, "your name is

being Raymond Parson. You work for the Metro Export-Import Company of Alexandria, Virginia. You are just returning from business trip to Cyprus, Greece.''

"That's right.''

The man cocked his head and gave me a sly look. I decided I better not fall into the trap of thinking the man stupid. And there was the blond man by the door. He looked as though he might have a speck of brain up there between his ears. I figured I'd better cut the jokes and play it serious.

"Now that you've invaded the privacy of an honest American citizen,'' I said, turning to look at each of the four men in turn, ''perhaps you'll be kind enough to tell me what this is all about, or get the hell out of here. I really don't want to call the police unless it's necessary.''

"It isn't necessary,'' the blond said. He smiled.

"The point is, Mr. Parson, we don't believe you. Even if we did, we have our orders. You are to come with us. If you are not Nick Carter, you will be released unharmed.''

I gazed at the handsome man with the straw-colored hair. I placed the accent as pure Muscovite. And there was intelligence and education in the voice, the choice of words. I had long ago pegged all four men as KGB. And I'd learned long ago not to let the stupid members of the Russian secret police lull me into a false belief that all KGB men were brainless apes. Even the CIA had its losers; that was one of the rationales for an organization like AXE.

Jesus, it hit me. How in the world did these men know of Nick Carter? And did they know of AXE, the most secret of all espionage agencies in the whole world? No, impossible. They'd said nothing about AXE. Then again, they'd said very little except to call me Nick Carter and insist that I come with them.

I thought I knew where they were taking me. The Soviet Embassy. If so, perhaps there was hope. No, I couldn't bring in the American Embassy to help a man named Raymond Parson. If anyone—Americans or Russians—began to dig into my cover, they'd know that something was fishy. Too much digging would bring Hawk screaming out of his little nest down on Dupont Circle and then all hell would break loose.

As usual, Nick Carter was on his own. Whatever this problem was, I'd have to get out of it myself—alone.

"All right," I said, slipping on my jacket and facing the blond man. "I'm too tired to argue the finer points of this fiasco. Let's get going and settle this real quick."

"Thank you, Mr. Carter—er, Parson," the blond man said. "I had hoped you would see things our way. We shall conduct ourselves as gentlemen and, as you say, settle this real quick."

As we rode along Washington's dark, almost deserted streets, I relaxed in the rear seat of the big Lincoln limo. I'd noticed the license plate when we'd come out of the apartment building. Embassy plates. I'd guessed right—they were taking me to the Russian Embassy.

The blond man gave me a cigarette as the limo eased noiselessly down Rhode Island Avenue toward Scott Circle. I'd left my special Turkish jobs, with my initials "NC" in gold, with my weapons and my other paraphernalia, so I was dying for a smoke. I took the cigarette, watched the man's face as he lit it with a Bic lighter. He was smiling in the dark rear seat.

"I have a feeling," I said, as the car entered Scott Circle and I began to hope it wouldn't swing right, up Massachusetts Avenue, along Embassy Row, "that you won't be smiling long, my friend. Once you realize that you've kidnapped an ordinary American citizen, you'll find just how *extraordinary* ordinary American citizens are. Your ass, to put it crudely, will be in one really big sling."

He snapped off the Bic, saying nothing. I would have bet that most of that smile was gone. I watched as the limo passed Massachusetts Avenue, and breathed easier. The Soviet Embassy wasn't on Embassy Row with so many others. The Russkies, for some reason, had located only four blocks up from the White House, on Sixteenth Street between Burlington and L. Don't get me wrong—I was far from happy about being dragged from my bed of exhaustion and hauled off to the Soviet Embassy. But I knew that if they took me to one of the satellite-country embassies, I might never emerge from it alive. In the perverse thinking of the Soviets, it was thought that the Mother embassy could be kept clean by having all the dirty work done in the satellite digs.

The driver, one of the two thugs who'd put my bed together and then torn my apartment apart, hung a right on Sixteenth. Ahead was the big neon sign of the Statler-Hilton. The Soviet Embassy was a block short of that, across from the National Geographic Society buildings. Okay, the Russians were fielding this one themselves, whatever it was. I could at least hope for a clean act, or reasonably so.

Then again, what choice did I have? Even if there weren't four of them, my body was too far shot to make a fight of it. I'd thought of making a run for it when we'd come out of my apartment building, but my legs were having none of that. When they didn't respond to my first mental impulse to run like blazes, my mind gave up, issuing no further silly orders like that.

The embassy building was dark on the outside, but lights blazed indoors. The two goons and the ugly man with the garlic breath seemed to disappear into the woodwork. The blond man who was fond of smiling and sounding erudite led me up a flight of stairs to the second floor. In a large, comfortable-looking office, he motioned me to an overstuffed chair and I collapsed into it. He sat behind a huge desk.

"Now, Mr. Carter or Mr. Parson," he said, the smile back, "let us play the popular American game 'Twenty Questions.' " Before I could respond he began the barrage. How long was I in Russia? What parts of Russia did I visit? How did I get into and out of the country without the authorities knowing? How many innocent Soviet citizens did I deprive of their lives? Why did I kill these innocent Soviet citizens? What organization was behind me? When did I plan to return to start the killing again?

"Know something?" I said, summoning up enough strength for one more shot at this guy. "I pegged you as being a bit on the bright side when you first opened your yap. Boy, was I wrong."

He smiled. "Mr. Carter, if you don't answer my questions, I'm afraid I'll have to summon my men and let them interrogate in their own inimitable style. We don't want that, do we, Mr. Carter?"

"The name is Parson."

He leaned forward, his face stern. "Enough with the charade. I will give you five more minutes of my time unless you begin to respond to my queries. After that, we'll see just how extraordinary this ordinary American citizen really is. Mikhail and the others are literally itching for me to turn you over to them."

I sighed. "Look, I think the time has come for you to let me talk to the ambassador or one of his deputies. I—"

"My name is Ivan Pavolovitch Zygorsky," he said, the way a student would commence a memorized recitation. "I am first deputy to the Soviet Emissary. The emissary and the ambassador are both out of the country. So you see, Mr. Carter/Parson, you are now talking to the highest-ranking official at the embassy. Now, one other question and I will leave you alone for five minutes to come up with some answers. There is only one way you could have gone into Russia, did what you did and come out again. You had help, a pipeline. Not only help from whatever organization you represent here in America, but from disloyal spies within Russia. I want names, dates, places, Mr. Carter."

He stood up, took a yellow legal pad and a pen from his desk. He came around and put them in my lap.

"I'm certain that a man of your qualifications will have no trouble recalling the questions I have asked. Write your answers on the pad. In five minutes, Mikhail and his friends will return. If the pad is empty, well, let us say that you've been warned. Goodnight, Mr. Carter/Parsons. I too am exhausted."

With that, he left the room. I stared at the pad. As tired as I was, I remembered his questions. They were gonging like churchbells in my head and my mind kept screaming at me: "What the fuck is that madman talking about?"

After four minutes, the door opened. I turned, expecting to see the ugly face of the man named Mikhail. It was Ivan; he had a strange look on his face and carried a Manila envelope in his right hand. He walked past me and stood behind his desk. He gazed at me for a full minute, then began to shake his head back and forth, slowly, slowly.

"You have incredible luck, Mr. Parson," he said. "I had

already told Mikhail and his team to come fetch you when something really important came over our special network from Moscow. I will show it to you.''

He took a sheet of flimsy paper from the Manila envelope. I could see that the front side was covered by something very dark, in computer ink. He slid it across the desk, face down. I picked it up and turned it over.

It was a very grainy photograph of a man in a crazy-quilt khaki uniform. He was a fairly young man, perhaps thirty. He was kneeling in the open doorway of a barn loft. He held a high-powered .30 caliber rifle in his hands. And he looked as though he was totally unaware that his picture was being taken.

"Do you know this man?" Zygorsky asked.

"Would you believe me if I said that I didn't?"

He nodded, smiled. "Yes, Mr. Parson, I would believe you. I can tell you one thing and one thing only. The man in the picture is Nick Carter. And now, I apologize for having inconvenienced you. My men will return you to your apartment and make things as right as possible. I would ask that you not make an issue of what has happened tonight. Please forget it. You see, as far as I am concerned,'' and he shrugged and smiled broadly now, "nothing happened tonight. Nothing at all.''

His word was good. Mikhail and his two goons returned me to my apartment, the three of them put everything back together and left.

I sat on the side of the bed, my head spinning with questions. I should call David Hawk, my boss, call him at home. I should find out who that man in the picture was. I should find out what he was doing to make the Russians track me down like this. I should find out how the Russians had tracked me down. I should. . .

Before I knew it I was sound asleep.

TWO

The drugstore on the corner of Florida and Georgia Streets, across from Howard University's field house, wasn't crowded at two in the afternoon. Few places are at that time of the day. But I dawdled over my fourth cup of coffee and tried to decide what to do.

They were watching me. The big Lincoln limo was parked across Florida, in broad daylight. In the back seat was Mikhail, the ugly ape who'd opened the wound in my shoulder last night; his two goons were in front.

My first indication that the Russians weren't really through with me was when I'd awakened just after noon, taken another shower and picked up the phone to call David Hawk. The hollow sound, the faint buzz and click, told me the phone to my safehouse was being tapped. A call to Metro Export-Import would have been legitimate for a man named Raymond Parson. But the call would have been redirected by special computer to Hawk's office number on Dupont Circle.

We would have had to talk about the export-import business. I couldn't have told Hawk the real reason for my call. Instead I had dialed the number for the correct time and weather report, learned that it was 12:46 and that it was eighty-two degrees outside in sunny Maytime Washington, then had hung up. And then, hunger overcoming me again, I had gotten my little Dodge Aries out of the apartment garage and driven to this drugstore for breakfast.

Not ten feet from me was a telephone booth and I knew it

was a safe phone. But Mikhail and his goons were watching. I didn't want them to see me make a call and then to follow me to AXE headquarters. Since there really was a Metro, I toyed with the idea of going all the way to Alexandria and having Hawk come there. I needed some answers that only he could get for me.

But, if I went to Alexandria and Hawk came there, the Russians would spot him and start putting more pieces together. I didn't want to add more to the picture they already had. Hell, maybe they knew it all—about me and AXE and David Hawk and the other agents. No, Ivan had let me go, had said the soldier boy in the barn loft was Nick Carter. Then again, he'd had me followed.

Making things worse, my shoulder was throbbing, my head was pounding and I still yearned for more sleep. That Cyprus caper had nearly done me in. That and the nightmare with the Russians.

Still, I had to do something. With them following me, a meeting with Hawk was out, so I'd have to do it all over the phone. Dangerous, but necessary. I snaked twenty cents out of my pocket, glanced across the street at the big limo and walked slowly to the phone booth. I closed the door and dialed a number that would drive the Russians crazy if they tried to trace it.

Computers clicked and hummed and rustled about in computer whispers, then Hawk was on the line.

"What's going on, N3? Why weren't you here at nine for a complete debriefing on Cyprus? Where are you?"

"Got a new problem," I said. "I'll write up my report on Cyprus and leave it at the Georgetown drop for someone to pick up. Basically, though, it went well and the problem has been dissolved."

"Good, what's next?"

"Some Snowmen routed me last night," I told him. "Snowmen" was the code word for Russians.

He grunted and I knew that he was chewing on a cigar.

"Look, I can't explain everything in code, boss," I said, thinking of all that had happened last night, "so I'll give it to you straight. I'm being followed, so I won't come near your place."

"Sounds interesting. Are you certain the phone is safe?"

"As safe as any phone in Washington." I told him all about last night, from the brutal awakening in my apartment, to the ride over to Sixteenth and L, to the nutsy questions about me just returning from Russia, to the showing of the picture of a man in a soldier suit. I added Ivan Zygorsky's veiled threat about making a fuss.

"But the main point is that they received a picture of a man they say is Nick Carter. And this Carter is—or was—in Russia killing people. On the strength of that picture, and the fact that I don't look anything like the man in the makeshift soldier suit, they let me go. But they're still following me, have my apartment phone bugged and I'd damned well like to know how the hell they got onto me in the first place."

"Have you been to your regular apartment?"

"Yeah. I went there as soon as I got off the plane to dump my identity papers and weapons and other stuff. I haven't been back, though, if that's what you mean."

"Don't go there. Stay where you are and let me do some checking."

"I can't stay in this drugstore. I'm highly exposed and I can't eat another bite. I'll cruise around, try to lose these suckers and call you back."

"Right. Give me an hour, to the minute."

I checked my watch as I hung up. Two nineteen. I paid for my breakfast, walked casually to my car and pulled out onto Florida, moving at a leisurely pace downtown. I zigged and zagged around the Capitol Building, circled the Mall, drove past the White House and the Soviet Embassy, circled Scott Circle three times and then set off up Massachusetts Avenue. I would lose the Russians in Georgetown.

Thirty minutes later, after miraculously escaping getting stopped by vigilant Washington traffic cops, I had lost them. I even cruised back past the Soviet Embassy to make sure. Once I was confident they were no longer tailing me, I headed back up Rhode Island toward my regular apartment.

Hawk had warned me not to go there, but I felt really naked without my weapons. I circled the building several times and then parked four blocks away, walking a circuitous route back. The apartment was clean. The tiny sliver of plastic I'd put in the door jamb was still there. So were the three long black hairs beneath the door. And so was the bit of tape over the keyhole.

And so were my beloved weapons.

I took off my jacket, carefully because my right shoulder was still sending urgent signals to my pain centers, and strapped on Wilhelmina, nestling the 9mm Luger tightly under my left armpit. Next, I strapped the leather sheath carrying Hugo, the razor-sharp stiletto, to my right wrist, then dropped my pants. Once Pierre the gas bomb was nestled in its little lambskin pouch behind my testicles, I dressed, left the apartment and put all the tape, plastic and hair back in place.

At precisely 3:17, I walked back into the same drugstore where I'd had breakfast. I figured Mikhail to be bright enough to know that no spy would ever return to the place he'd been when he'd spotted his tail. But not bright enough to know that most spies frequently go against such implacable rules.

I called Hawk and listened to an incredible story—and it wasn't even the whole story.

Two weeks ago, a political officer—or commissar—in Kharkov, a city in the Ukrainian S.S.R., was killed by a high-powered rifle bullet to the head. The following morning, the local KGB office received a note in English, claiming that the commissars of the province were corrupt and had to die. The note was signed: ''Nick Carter, American espionage agent.''

In the following nine days, five more commissars were killed in the same manner, and five more notes signed by Nick Carter were left at KGB office doorsteps. The Russians were going out of their minds. They were losing some of their most important high-ranking party officials, whose job it was to oversee every aspect of Soviet life.

Hawk didn't know how KGB or Embassy people had gotten onto my trail, but it seemed that the American doing the killing of commissars used Cyprus as a route in and out of southern Russia. A KGB agent had trailed him two days ago to Cyprus, lost him and then, lo and behold, along came the real Nick Carter—and the KGB agent sent a dispatch to pick me up when I arrived in Washington.

Fortunately for me, the dispatch was late arriving at the Soviet Embassy and I had already dropped off my weapons and other materials before the pickup team made it to National Airport. But the team leader, Ivan Pavolovitch Zygorsky, checked the passenger manifest on the last flight from Cyprus and concluded that Raymond Parson was their man.

Now, what saved my butt last night was the fact that, on his last kill, the man calling himself Nick Carter was accidentally photographed when KGB men were out in the countryside with cameras with telescopic lenses. The man who took the photo didn't know what he had until the film was developed and blown up.

Unfortunately for me, the man calling himself Nick Carter had slipped back into Russia before I left Cyprus and made another kill. Since the picture was so grainy, it was impossible to make a positive identification. I wasn't being completely ruled out and that was why I was still being followed.

"It's best to let them keep you in sight," Hawk concluded. "If the killer strikes again, they'll rule you out and you'll be safe."

"But what about—ah, our little organization? Won't they keep sniffing until they come across certain facts that could blow our cover sky high?"

"Not likely," Hawk said, mumbling as though he were lighting a cigar. "My sources say the Russians are convinced that this Nick Carter who's killing the commissars is either CIA or some crackpot off on his own. Either way, we're out of it."

"You," I said. "I'm not out of it."

"You will be as soon as this nut kills somebody else."

"Chief, I think you're taking this whole thing pretty calmly," I blurted into the phone. "Jesus, there's a guy using my name going around killing people in Russia. Even if AXE is safe, there's still the possibility of an international incident that could blow—"

"My sources don't think so. As soon as the Russians

knock off the killer, they'll let the whole thing drop."

"Okay," I said, "but it still doesn't tell us who this guy is or why he's doing what he's doing. And it doesn't tell us how he knows about me—Nick Carter—being an espionage agent."

"Forget it, N3," Hawk snorted. "I know what you're thinking. Just to solve a little mystery, you want to charge off to Russia and catch this joker. And that, my friend, would blow things sky high."

"Chief, you and I both know that the Russians have a weird sense of logic. Sooner or later, they're going to get tired of the game and decide that I'm somehow linked with the nut who's killing their political officers. When that happens, they'll blow me away like so much soot. And if the guy isn't caught, if he continues to kill, his exploits will gain international attention. If that happens, digging will start in earnest. We might find ourselves in the spotlight. I think I should get over there and—"

"I'll be in touch," he said, abruptly cutting me off.

He'd already hung up before I could say more. I stood there with the dead phone, feeling like a fool. How was he going to get back to me if he didn't even know where I was? I hadn't given him the name of the drugstore, or the phone number of the paybooth.

I decided to give him an hour and then I would call back. I stepped up to the counter, nodded to the cute little waitress who was already beginning to look like an old friend and ordered a cup of coffee.

As I drank, I felt as though I were being watched. I turned slowly on the stool, looked through the open front door and, *voilà*, there they were: Mikhail and his goons in the big Lincoln limo.

My mind ticked off my options. I could wait the hour and call Hawk back—knowing full well that, no matter what he came up with, I had to go to Russia. I could take off again and shake the tail. Or, I could go out and confront Mikhail and ask him why he was still on my case.

The only option that seemed to make sense was to wait. Hawk must have somehow discovered where I was or he wouldn't have said he'd get back to me. I figured it to be a long, dreary hour of waiting, and I hoped my kidneys and my nerves could stand all the coffee I'd be drinking.

As it turned out, I didn't have an hour. More like twenty minutes.

And what happened, happened so fast that I wasn't sure what was going down until it was almost over.

Shortly before four o'clock, I heard the squeal of tires as several cars sped up to the intersection. I whirled about on the stool, expecting to see a whole platoon of Russian soldiers pouring out onto the street. What I saw was five ordinary cars, unmarked as to official attachment, filling the intersection. Two cars had the Lincoln hemmed at the curbing. Two were pointed at the limo from the center of the intersection, like two rockets ready to go off. The fifth car was directly outside the drugstore.

Plainclothesmen were spilling out of the five cars. I didn't recognize any of them, but they were big men, very athletic-looking, and quite determined to carry out whatever mission they'd been assigned. I saw pistols flash into view, saw the doors of the Lincoln being opened, saw the Russian goons being yanked out onto the street.

And then three men in the nearest car were storming through the doors of the drugstore. They looked around, saw that no other customers were in the place and headed for me. One of them produced a piece of cloth that looked exactly like a bag. Head-sized.

The cute waitress behind the counter yelped and all three men put their fingers to their lips, then pocketed their handguns. Two of them grabbed my arms and pinned them to my sides. I'd been so intent on what was happening to Mikhail and his friends that I hadn't even gone for a weapon.

"Hey, what the hell do you think you're doing?" I shouted.

"Shut up," one of the men hissed. And then the bag flapped like the crack of a whip and went over my head. "Don't struggle," the man with the bag whispered, "or we'll have to konk you one."

I struggled.

One foot managed to find a set of testicles somewhere out there in the darkness and a man yelped like a woman. The waitress screamed again, and again there were shushing sounds. Outside on the street, muffled by the thickness of the cloth bag, there were yelps and howls and protests. Horns blew as normal motorists tried to get through the jammed intersection. From a distance, a police siren wailed.

Before I could kick again, strong hands and arms wrapped around me and lifted me off the floor. I felt myself being carried, in an upright position. Next thing I knew, a door was being opened and, in spite of my kicking and yelling, I was thrust into the back seat of a car.

The commotion at the intersection of Florida and Georgia was still going on when the car sped away with a squeal of tires. At least five G's pressed me back against the soft seat and I stopped struggling. I'd managed only to revive the excruciating pain in my shoulder.

About ten minutes later I felt that the car was crossing a bridge. There was that peculiar sound of wheel noise being bounced back by a bridge abutment. Across the bridge, one of the men pulled the bag off my head. I coughed, took a deep breath and looked my kidnappers in the face.

The man I'd kicked in the nuts was driving, obviously still in pain. He was giving me looks through the rearview mirror. The men on either side of me were grinning, their hands in their laps, but seemingly ready for swift action if I didn't behave as ordered. The pistols were out of sight, tucked neatly in underarm holsters.

"Well," I said, trying to sound chipper. "That was a nice way to start a party. What now?"

"Now," a blue-eyed man on my left said, still grinning, "the party spreads out. You go one way, we go another."

"I see. And which way do I go?"

The man kept on grinning. "Wherever the Air Force has orders to take you," he said. "Frankly, Mac," he continued, "we don't know very much about what's going down. We got a call from somebody very high up, had a quick briefing on the situation, were told to put the muscle to some goons in a Lincoln limo and to hustle the guy in the drugstore off to Andrews Air Force Base. Beyond that, it's as much mystery to us as it is to you. All I can say is that you fit the description we were given of the man who would be in the drugstore."

An hour later, I was aboard a huge Air Force transport plane with a bunch of jeeps, heading for England. Now I pulled out the thick envelope the blue-eyed man had pressed in my hand, broke the seal and removed the note.

"You were right. Locate and eliminate. We won't rest easy until you do."

It was signed with a single initial: "H."

H for Hawk.

Also in the envelope was a packet of good old American greenbacks. I was fast asleep among the jeeps before I could count the stuff.

THREE

I dozed, my head lightly jostling against the window of the AirTurk DC-10 bound from London to Ankara. In spite of the long layover and the lovely hotel room in London, I was still weary. I figured it would take a month to catch up on sleep lost during that Cyprus caper.

I was barely aware that someone had slipped into the empty seat beside me. But the delicious-smelling perfume soon penetrated my olfactory nerve and I knew that the newcomer was a woman. I didn't move or look at her right away, although I was more awake than asleep. It was nice to keep my eyes closed and think about things.

The Air Force had provided a car to Heathrow Airport in London after the transport had touched down. A lieutenant had stayed with me while I took a short nap at the airport hotel, then had shared drinks with me in the bar until my Ankara flight was announced. I'd decided it was too risky returning to Cyprus, and I couldn't get a flight to eastern Turkey. From Ankara, I'd have to catch a bus or a train to Hopa, a seacoast town near the Russian border. My definite plans didn't go beyond that point.

The plane to Ankara was only half full, so there was room to spread out. I'd had a whole three-seat parcel all to myself until we were somewhere over Luxembourg. And then the perfume-laden woman had joined me, taking the aisle seat.

As the plane passed over Austria, the white-capped Alps far, far below, I decided finally to sneak a peek.

She was gorgeous, and she was filing already perfect nails

with an intensity that made her lips seem to pout with gamine mischief. Her legs were crossed and the split in her clinging jersey dress had fallen away to reveal a perfect thigh covered by delicately tinted silk stockings.

I pretended to wake up then, yawning, looking about. Naturally, my sleepy, searching eyes lit on hers. She had wide hazel eyes, so lambent and moist that I felt that I could dive in and swim about.

"Hello," she said cheerily, those lovely eyes and lips unfolding like a beautiful flower into a most devastating smile. "Hope you don't mind if I sit here. I'm trying to escape from a dirty old man with roaming hands."

"Soon's I come awake," I said, faking another yawn, "I'll go punch the old geezer out."

She laughed. I'd expected something delicate and bell-like from this lovely doll, but her laughter was husky, throaty, a combination of Tallulah Bankhead and Lauren Bacall. She pushed back a hank of reddish brown hair and smiled into my eyes. I smiled back into hers, knowing I wouldn't find girlish innocence there, but surprised at what I did find.

Fear.

The girl was afraid, but not of some grabbing, pinching, ogling plane partner. The fear went deeper, had been there longer than it had taken the plane to fly from London to Austria, and would be there long after she departed the plane in Ankara.

"You must have been really tired," she said, breaking the eyelock and gazing at the window behind me. "You sleep as though you aren't afraid of anything in the world. Me, I sleep like a trapped bunny, all senses alert for the prowling fox."

I didn't tell her about the nightmares that haunted my sleep, or the ever-present threats I encountered in my waking hours as Killmaster for AXE. And I wondered if she'd seen any kind of fear in my eyes when we'd exchanged that electrifying stare. The fear was there. I had been inside Russia before on assignments; I didn't relish going back. And, with my shoulder working at less than fifty percent and the Russians on to me because of a phony Nick Carter out killing commissars, I really had no business going to Russia. Not now.

We discussed sleeping habits a bit more, then I asked her

destination.

The fear twittered in her eyes, in spite of her open smile. "Well, it certainly isn't Ankara," she said lightly. "I've heard it's the pits."

My turn to laugh. "True, but we're heading for the part of the world that's always been the pits and always will be."

"You mean Turkey?"

"Turkey, Greece, the whole Middle East and, of course, the big dark land that lies like a blot on the map out there beyond the Black Sea."

"Goodness, don't tell me you're going to Russia," she said. Fear fairly danced in her eyes. And something else. Hope? Expectation? I couldn't tell.

"Not if I can help it," I lied. "Are you going to Russia?"

She shook her head, but her eyes told me something else. "I have a friend in Hopa, a seacoast town near the Russian border. That's as close as I want to get to Mother Russia."

Hopa. I was heading for Hopa. Had this girl known it when she came to sit with me? Was the story of the dirty old man a lie? Was this girl a KGB pointer? If she were, the Russians were upgrading their personnel mightily.

"I'll be traveling much of Turkey," I said. "My first stop will be Trabzon."

"Wonderful," she said, shifting in the seat and clapping her hands, letting the slit dress fall away to reveal flesh almost to her crotch. "That's only a hundred miles this side of Hopa. Maybe we can travel together until we get to Trabzon."

"Suits me just fine," I said, eyeballing the thigh in spite of my pledge not to. "But, if you don't like devouring eyes, you'd better do something about that skirt." Her smile just about melted the bandage on my shoulder. "There are some people," she said enticingly, "who I don't mind looking." She put her hand on one of mine. "I don't even know your name and I think you're one of those people."

I introduced myself as Raymond Parson. She told me her name was Tania Koselke, and I found out later that the name was her real one.

"Well, Tania," I said, "tell me more about this friend in Hopa and why you're going so close to a country you obviously fear."

The friend, she said, had been with her in the Peace Corps at one time. She fell in love with a Turkish boy and married him. The Turk was a lawyer who had returned to his hometown to set up practice. A simple story, but I didn't believe a word of it. There was the fear in this girl's lovely eyes—and something else that I couldn't put my finger on.

As for myself, I gave my present cover with Metro Export-Import and knew as I talked that she didn't believe a word I was telling her. For the moment, we both let it drop.

"Do you have a place to stay in Ankara?" she finally asked.

"No. I'd hoped to get a bus or train right away. I have a meeting first thing in the morning and—"

"This is your first trip this way, isn't it?"

I didn't answer immediately; I didn't know how to. As an exporter salesman, I should have been over this territory like a glove. But then, there was a first time for everything.

"I haven't been with Metro long," I lied—and didn't lie. "Why do you ask?"

"Because we'll arrive in Ankara after midnight and there are no buses or trains heading east and north until tomorrow. And, with the increased traffic and the slowness of the Turks to take advantage of tourism, you'll never get a hotel room unless you have a reservation."

I grinned. "Maybe the airline will let me snooze right here until the trains and buses start to run."

"Maybe," she said, grinning slyly. "Then, again, perhaps they won't. In any event, you're welcome to share my room. I reserved one with twin beds."

Generally speaking, only a damned fool would have turned down such an invitation from a beautiful, sexy, woman. But something told me this girl was no innocent tourist on her way to meet an old Peace Corps friend. KGB? Possible, but I doubted it. CIA? Possible, even probable. Had Hawk's sources talked the old man into sending some unlikely agent to keep an eye on me? No. If the girl were CIA, she was acting on orders quite independent of AXE.

But that still didn't explain the depthless fear in those lovely eyes. This girl was on a mission that somehow scared the hell out of her. Perhaps that mission had nothing to do with me. Perhaps she'd sought me out as company to help eliminate some of her own fear, whatever it was. I even began to doubt that there was a dirty old man on the plane, a man whose actions had forced her to change her seat.

And I was right. After we landed at Ankara—and it was decided that I'd share her room with the twin beds—we were going up the aisle together when a little old lady looked up from a seat and touched Tania's arm.

"I missed you when I woke up, dear," the old lady said sweetly, looking at both of us with a knowing eye, "but I see you were in good hands. Have a nice journey on to Hopa."

Tania blushed and said goodbye to the old woman. Off the plane, walking across the tarmac to the low terminal, she took my wrist and looked up at me.

"Sorry about the little white lie," she said. "The truth is, I was lonely. When Thelma went to sleep, I looked around for someone to talk to."

"You forget," I said, knowing I might blow the whole deal by speaking the truth now, "I was also asleep."

She smiled. "Yes, but I knew both of you would wake up. Given a choice, I chose you."

Flattery, they say, breaks down many barriers, will get you anything. In this case, it almost got me killed.

After we'd picked up our baggage and were waiting on the platform for a taxi to the hotel, Tania gripped my wrist again. Hard.

"Mr. Parson," she said, her breath whistling through her gleaming white teeth, "a man has been following us all the way from the gate. Don't look now, but he's standing by that column at the bus stop. When you get the chance, peek and see if you know who he is."

I nodded, looked at my watch and told her the time, as though that was what she'd asked for. In the same movement, I let my eyes flicker over the guy by the stone column. I didn't know him, but I knew his type: short with a homely face, padded shoulders on the cheap suit, a battered fedora, scuffed shoes and a bulge under his left arm.

KGB.

My heart sank. How could they have traced me here? If they'd been looking for me to sneak into Russia, they'd expect me to turn up in Cyprus, certainly not central Turkey.

I had to find out just how rigid the trap really was. I turned slowly, pretending to look for a taxi, and saw a second man standing by another column to our left. Behind us, just inside the glass doors, was another. I leaned down to Tania.

"Nothing to worry about," I said. "My boss warned me that the Turkish secret police watches all newcomers, especially Americans. Let's pretend we don't notice them, get the taxi and go to the hotel. If we don't do anything suspicious, they'll do no more than watch."

"They?" she asked, her eyes flaring. "There's more than one?"

I told her about the guy to our left and the guy behind. I took her hand to prevent her from squirreling around to look. A taxi was coming.

"Ignore them," I said. "Pretend they're not . . ."

Tania bolted away from me as the three men made their move. They were coming toward us, walking rapidly, purposefully. Tania broke and ran across the empty street, toward the parking lot. I knew that running was the worst thing for either of us to do, but my legs suddenly whipped into action and I was running after Tania.

The three men were drawing weapons behind us, just starting to run. Tania made it to the gate in the chain link fence around the parking lot and turned to stare at me, and at the onrushing men. Her eyes literally sparked with fear.

In that moment, two huge buses rumbled down the wide street between us and the three men. The taxi, angry that the buses had cut it away from the platform, came veering around, close to us. I whistled, raised my arm, waved my hand. The taxi driver hit the brakes.

"Come on," I yelled at Tania, pulling her arm. "Let's get out of here."

She hesitated, hanging onto the fence, then let go. I opened the door, pushed her inside and jumped in after her. The buses had stopped and I saw the three men circling around them. Tania was frozen in the rear seat, her hands clutched at her mouth.

"Tell the driver the name of your hotel," I shouted. "Hurry."

The three men spotted us and broke out their pistols. The

cabdriver, watching Tania and her exposed leg, didn't see the men or the guns.

"Downtown," I yelled at the cabbie. "Hurry, take us downtown." I felt a moment of panic, wondering if the guy spoke or understood English.

"Hokay, Jake," he blurted, grinning with big yellow teeth and taking the twenty dollar bill I poked at him.

Before he could get turned around and set the cab in motion, one of the three men fired. I saw the tongue of flame and then heard the splintering of safety glass as the bullet plunged through the right window, grazing the back of my head.

"Holy Jakes," the cabbie yelped. "What. . ."

I had Wilhelmina in my hand. I'd been trying to decide whether to return the fire from the men, decided instead to use it to get us some speed. I stuck the cold barrel against the cabbie's head.

"Downtown. Hurry. Now!"

His foot hit the accelerator just as another tongue of flame burst from a gun twenty feet from the rear of the taxi. I was starting to duck when the force of the takeoff slammed me into the rear seat. I sprawled across the frightened Tania, felt all kinds of naked flesh rubbing against me, almost lost my grip on Wilhelmina.

By the time I'd recovered my balance and looked through the rear window where a neat hole was planted dead center, we were making a tight turn around the parking lot. I couldn't see the three men, but knew they were hurrying to cars somewhere back there.

We were halfway to the downtown section before Tania came out of her trance of fear enough to give the taxi driver the name of the hotel. The man, who'd seemed happy to see us when we'd first hailed his cab, was giving us both dour looks now. He'd inspected the damage to his machine and knew that twenty American bucks wouldn't cover a fraction of it.

"How much English do you understand?" I asked as I put my Luger away.

"Know plenty English, Jake," he said. "Know take plenty money for fixing windows."

"All right," I said. "I'll take care of that." I slipped him five more twenties and his eyes goggled like the lights on a pinball machine. "Now I want to take care of something else. You forget the name of the hotel the lady just gave you, okay?" I gave him another twenty.

"Hokay, Jake. Already forgot."

"Take us to the bus station," I said.

He swiveled to look at me. At the same time, Tania gripped my arm. "Bus station closed, Jake," the driver said.

"I know. Now, I also know that you're wondering why those guys were shooting at us. Right?"

"Not my problem now," he said. "Nobody hit. Plenty money to fix up."

"You'll be asked where you took us," I said. "Tell them the truth—the bus station. If they start to get nasty and ask about the hotel, stay mum until it looks as though you might be hurt. Make them pay and then give them the name the lady gave you. Can you remember it?"

He turned and broke into that yellow-toothed grin again. "Never forgot, Jake. Was lying."

I gave him two more twenties and settled back alongside Tania. She was trembling like a windup toy gone bonkers. I put my arm around her, to settle her. She put her face against my shoulder and cried.

She cried all the way to the dark bus station.

"We'll find another hotel," I said. "And we have a hell of a lot of talking to do. I want to know who you really are and why you're here and where you're going."

"But I told—"

"You told me lies and I told you lies," I snapped. "From now on, we play it square or I leave you standing right here. I've finally figured it out, beautiful."

"Figured what out?"

"Those men weren't Turkish secret police. They were KGB, as I'd first pegged them. And they weren't looking for me. They were after you. I want to know why, or this relationship goes no further. Fair enough?"

She took a deep breath, let it out with a shudder and nodded.

"Get us to a hotel," she said, "and I'll tell you the whole story."

It cost me a hundred dollars in bribes to get a room with a big double bed.

I hoped it would be worth it.

FOUR

Her name really was Tania Koselke. She had been born in
Indianapolis, Indiana, of an Irish mother and a Russian
father. The father, Itzchak Koselkovitch, had escaped from
Russia in 1956, just after the Hungarian revolution. As a
political escapee, he was given asylum, a new identity—
Zeke Koselke—and a job in the Midwest.

In Indianapolis, Zeke met Sharon Shannon, pure Irish.
They were married within a month, but Tania wasn't born
until 1963.

"All my life," she said, "my father talked about my
Russian relatives. His father and mother, his brothers and
sisters, nieces, nephews, cousins, aunts and uncles. They all
live in the Kharkov-Rostov area in the southern Ukraine and
northern Caucasus. I decided a year ago that I would someday visit them, even though my father is against the idea.
Three months ago, I applied for a visa, but the Russians
turned me down. In fact, my actions caused them to check
into my family and I nearly got my father into trouble."

"And," I said as we sat in the hotel room's two comfort-
able chairs, "in spite of all that, you still intend to go to
Russia."

"Yes." She looked at me and I saw that she was telling the
truth. The fear was still there, but it was understandable that
she'd be paranoid. Her father had reason to be; so had she. "I
know it's foolish, but I feel a bit like Alex Haley looking for
his roots. You see, all my mother's family are gone. She was

29

orphaned at the age of three. My Russian family is all I have outside my mother and father.''

''If they catch you,'' I said, ''you know what will happen?''

She shrugged pretty shoulders. I caught the gentle rise and fall of her heavy breasts and tried not to look. ''Throw me out, I suppose.''

''No. They'll keep you as a hostage and demand that your father return.''

The fear deepened in her eyes. Her chin went into a determined stance. ''I'll just have to make certain they don't catch me,'' she said.

I nodded, thinking of how she'd used me to get out of the airport, past those KGB agents she must have known would be waiting for her. I also remembered how she'd frozen with fear then.

''Tania,'' I said softly, ''once you're inside Russia, there won't be guys like me to bail you out of trouble. Which brings me to another point: How did you know I could help you when the plane touched down?''

''I didn't. But you looked so—well, so strong and self-controlled. You were the best catch on the plane. And it worked. You got me through.''

''Yeah, but how do you plan to get into Russia now that they're onto you?''

She smiled that devastating smile again, leaned forward and put the tip of her finger on the tip of my nose.

''Before we get into that, Mr. Raymond Parson,'' she said impishly, ''let's clear up your story. Just as you didn't believe my story about the old Peace Corps friend living in Hopa, I don't believe for a minute that you're a salesman for an export-import company. For one thing,'' she added, touching the lump that was Wilhelmina under my left arm, ''there's that wicked gun. And you also have some kind of weapon on your right wrist. I felt it back there at the airport.''

''You're right on all counts,'' I said, ''but it isn't what you're thinking. I'm armed because I mean business on what I have to do.''

''And what is that?''

I spun a reasonably believable yarn about having a brother

who'd gone to Russia on a visit three months ago, had been arrested in Moscow and was to be tried as a spy.

"I didn't bother applying for a visa," I said. "I don't want them to know I even exist or have any interest in what they do. But one way or the other, I'm going to get my innocent brother out of that prison."

I don't think she really believed me. To tell the truth, there were a few holes in both our stories. Oh, I was certain she was part Russian, part Irish. I was certain she had relatives in Russia. But there was something extra in her determination to visit them. I had the feeling that that something had more behind it than a curiosity to find roots. Especially after being shot at by KGB men who easily could have killed us both.

But we'd reached a kind of psychological standoff that prevented further questioning. If she didn't accept my story, she could expect me to probe into her story. And neither story would hold water for very long.

"It looks as though I made a good choice on that plane," she said, withering me with that smile again. "You're perfect in just about every way. Will you stay with me, help me get into Russia? Once we're inside, you can go your way and I'll go mine."

I really didn't need this kind of trouble. Getting in alone was going to be touchy at best. Taking on a girl who'd already been spotted by the KGB only made my job a few thousand percent harder. But I sure as hell couldn't abandon this beautiful babe-in-the-woods here in the middle of Ankara.

"Let's sleep on it," I said. "We're both tired and I always do my best thinking after a good night's sleep."

"All right."

She grabbed up her overnight bag and went into the bathroom. I quickly hid my weapons under the bed, then stripped down to my shorts. Fatigue began to work me over pretty good and I was half asleep when Tania finally came out, wearing an oversized man's tee-shirt.

The material was quite thin and I could see the outlines of her large pink nipples and reddish-brown pubes. The white material came to the middle of her thighs. She flashed her smile, then darted around the room to turn off the lights.

In the darkness, I could hear her unsteady breathing from across the room. I could almost sense her body trembling. It wasn't fear this time. It was desire. The room was full of it, and it wasn't all on Tania's part. I felt my own breathing coming in sharp, irregular little bursts. I felt my penis enlarging, swelling with that delicious warmth that spread from my loins up through my belly and chest. If I had had to scream then, no sound would have come. Lust had closed down my vocal cords for the night.

Even so, I decided not to leap to conclusions. The girl hadn't complained about the fact that we didn't have twin beds; she also hadn't made any promises. We simply hadn't discussed what we'd do when we were both in bed. The key word had been ''sleep.''

I heard her bare feet pad softly across the thin carpet, felt the covers being tugged back gently. I saw her silhouette from the faint light through the window. She stood beside the bed, watching me with unseen eyes. Suddenly, her hands grasped the hem of the tee-shirt and she slipped it off over her head. Her arm shot out and tossed the crumpled garment toward a dark chair.

Tania made a slow turn in the dim light from the street. I saw her large breasts, barely sagging. The nipples were taut and erect in silhouette. She sat on the edge of the bed and slid her legs beneath the covers so swiftly and silently that I wasn't sure she was in the bed. I lay still, listening to our combined breathing, feeling the throb in my groin as my prick turned from cement to pure steel.

Tania settled on her side of the bed with her back to me. Her perfume seemed to be stronger than it had been on the plane and I knew she'd given herself a generous lacing with it when she was in the bathroom. She wanted it, wanted it badly. I was just starting to reach out for her when she said, with startling clarity in the dark room:

''Good night, Mr. Parson.''

My whole body groaned. Steel reverted to stone, then to sagging flesh. My breathing became regular, normal. I turned to my left side, facing away from her.

''Good night, Tania Koselkovitch.''

Seconds ticked away, became minutes. For the first ten,

my body vibrated with the realization that a thoroughly
desirable, vulnerable and voluptuous young woman lay beside it, naked as a jaybird. Then, when her breathing sounded
regular, as though in sleep, the vibrations eased and I began
to drift off to sleep.

Nightmares started up immediately.

I was on a mountain ledge on a Caribbean island. Someone
from far below was firing automatic rifles up at the ledge.
Chunks of bullets and stones were flying all around me. I
started to move along the ledge, but there were sharp hunks of
metal all over the ledge. I knew that the metal shards were
coated with a potent poison. One nick from a sharp piece of
metal and the dying process would begin.

And then I was falling. I'd been chased to the edge of
another ledge, actually a cliff, and there were jungle trees
hundreds of feet below. I'd jumped to escape a squadron of
Cuban soldiers and the trees were looming closer and closer
as I fell.

A hand touched my stomach as I fell. The hand was warm,
soothing. I began to fall more slowly, actually floating. I
looked down, saw that I was naked. When I'd leaped from
the cliff, I'd been fully dressed in combat khakis. Now, I was
naked and this hand, this delicate feminine hand, was stroking my stomach. I began to erect.

The hand moved to my erection. The long fingers closed
around it and began a gentle stroking.

"Damn you, Parson," a soft voice said in my ear. "If you
won't take a subtle hint, then I'll have to make it an outright
offer."

With that, the covers flipped back and I opened my eyes in
time to see Tania Koselke's lithe body bend up and over me.
Her pendulant breasts brushed against my chest. Her long
auburn hair fell over my thighs. Her lips touched the bulging
head of my prick. Suddenly, her lips parted and she took me
into her mouth.

And that's how it began.

But not how it finished.

She was hungry, this Tania Koselke. She was also very
good. She brought me fully awake in a split second. The
aches and the exhaustion dissipated. Energy filled my veins

and muscles like pleasant charges of electricity.

When she came into my arms, she gasped at the touch of the bandage on my right shoulder. As our lips met in a wet, torrid kiss, her fingers traced the bandage so gently that I thought she had discovered some quick cure for wounds. I felt no pain there, not anywhere.

"There's more to you than you're telling," she whispered into my mouth. "But we'll worry about that in the morning."

And there was more to her than good looks. Her beauty went far beneath the skin, and so did I. When I slid into her, I felt as though I'd never stop, never reach the end of my adequacy.

The slow buildup took its toll, though. The whole thing was over too soon. I'd gone to sleep hotter than a desert cactus and the heat had never died off completely. When Tania came to me, when we joined, I was already past any normal man's endurance. I just felt lucky that I held off the explosion long enough for her to get her share of the final satisfaction. We exploded together.

Toward dawn, we awoke at the same time. We made love slowly, but with the same passion as before. When the second go-around was over, I had nothing left. I faded into a deep sleep like a rag that had been wrung out by strong hands.

There were no nightmares.

They didn't come until I awoke.

FIVE

The car was old and I worried that it wouldn't make it. I worried about a lot of things.

Tania and I had left the hotel before noon, but found the usual routes of escape cut off. When I scouted the bus station, there were the same KGB agents around that had been at the airport the night before. I tried the train station and found three clones of the first bunch.

I thought of finding the taxi driver who'd brought us from the airport, but there weren't enough twenties in the poke to get him to haul us all the way to Hopa.

So I rented a car. A 1957 Chevrolet, in fact. The body looked in fine shape, thanks to the fact that the Turks never use salt on their highways, but the engine sounded like an octogenarian dying of pneumonia.

Another worry. Tania had talked when we awoke, but I was still convinced that she wasn't telling everything. We were even in that department; I wasn't telling her everything, and she knew it.

Even so, we had hitched our wagons to each other, so to speak. We would enter Russia together, or die in the effort. I had this funny feeling as the ancient Chevy chugged along the bumpy, pockmarked highway to Hopa, that we'd more likely die.

The thought of entering Russia, coming after that late night rousting by the Soviet Embassy ''staff,'' made my stomach go queasy. I really didn't have much hope of finding the

American pseudo-soldier who was killing commissars and leaving my calling card at KGB offices.

Beyond that, even if I found him and killed him, what chance had I of getting out alive? The Russians, with their peculiar logic, wouldn't see me as a savior of any kind, but as an interloper, an intruder, a spy who'd cracked their border security. They'd happily kill or imprison me if they got their hands on me.

In spite of all my worries, and the extra burden of lovely Tania Koselke, I kept the old Chevy moving along, cringing when the wheezes and clunks began to sound mortal. My mind began to set priorities. If the car made it to Hopa, I'd try to bribe a fishing boat captain to slip us into Russia across the eastern tip of the Black Sea. Failing that, we'd try for a remote section of Russo-Turk border.

Even though Tania Koselke had singled me out as the man most likely to get her past trouble in Ankara, and I was fully aware that I was being used, I wanted to be used by this woman. I'd met and bedded a great number of women of varying ages in my career as Killmaster, but Tania seemed to have special ingredients in great supply. I could no sooner turn my back on her than I could leave my legs behind.

And despite the fact that the Russians were onto her and were out to stop her, the border guards most likely wouldn't be looking for a man and a woman. I doubted that the KGB men in Ankara had said much about last night's failure. They figured us to still be holed up in Ankara; they'd wait until they'd laid us low before reporting anything at all to Moscow. Of course, that theory wouldn't hold for long. Sooner or later, they'd have to report that Tania Koselke had slipped through their fingers with the help of an American man. We had to reach the border before they became that desperate.

With or without Tania, I couldn't turn back. My mind kept conjuring up that grainy picture of the blond man in the tattered khakis in the barn loft, the man with the high-powered rifle. How could he know of me? And why would he try to discredit me? And just how much did he know? If the Russians caught him, what could he tell them of Nick Carter and AXE? Maybe nothing. Then again, maybe enough to bring the whole secret organization tumbling to the ground.

All things considered, I had no choice but to keep my hands on the wheel, my foot on the juddering accelerator and my eyes on the rough road ahead. But my senses—virtually all of them—were on the lovely girl beside me.

"You never told me how you got hurt," Tania finally said. "Your shoulder."

A lie started to form in my mind. I decided to spice it with enough truth to make it believable.

"As you've guessed," I said, "I'm not a salesman. I work for the government."

"CIA?"

"No, just the government. I was on a mission in Greece when I learned about my brother, but I had to finish my mission before I could do anything about him. I'd been sent to Greece to eliminate a terrorist who was gaining too much power, thanks to help from Colonel Khaddafi of Libya. The terrorist and his followers were set to take over Cyprus. I made the kill, but had a little trouble escaping all in one piece. An American submarine was waiting for me in the Aegean. All I had to do was get to the end of a long pier, hop in a waiting speedboat and chug out to the rendezvous point."

"You obviously made it," Tania said, smiling at me as though she were happy I did. "What almost stopped you?"

"Groups of terrorists," I said, "are kind of like hydras— the many headed serpents. Kill one and another takes its place. Fortunately, the man who took over had far less brainpower than the leader I'd put away. But he had enough sense to set up mortar teams near that pier. I had to run the gauntlet through mortar blasts. A hunk of pier blew up too close to me and rammed a sharp splinter through my shoulder."

She seemed to ponder that a time. "That explains your nightmares?"

"What do you know about my nightmares?"

"I watched you sleeping," she said, gently, concerned. "The way you jerk and grunt and twist around, you must have some dillies. You even break out in sweat from time to time. And you mutter things."

I shrugged. "Nightmares are only nightmares," I said. "I can live with them."

"But how long can you live with the things that cause the nightmares? Experiences like running the gauntlet through mortar fire? And, I imagine, a lot of other fearsome adventures you must endure as a government man."

"You get an 'A' for astuteness and observation," I said, "but nothing more. I can't tell you who I really am or who I work for."

She smiled, nodded. She looked down at her hands and then at the road. I had the feeling that she had just made some kind of decision, some discovery. I started to ask her what she was thinking when the engine of the old Chevy gave one long wheeze and snort, and then died.

"What now?" she asked. She said it lightly, but the old fear was back in her voice. I wasn't the only one worried about events ahead of us.

"We're not far from Trabzon," I said. In fact, I could see the faint skyline of the fairly large town not three miles ahead. "Let's hope they have a mechanic who can put this dinosaur back into existence."

We walked into the seacoast city. It turned out to be five miles. I found a mechanic who was dirtier and greasier than the engines he worked on. After an exchange of only two twenties, he and an assistant chugged off in an ancient towtruck. Tania and I retreated to a cool tavern, sipped drinks and waited.

It was nearly dark when the mechanic came back into town, dragging the old Chevy along like a log he'd just retrieved from a prehistoric swamp. Fortunately, he said with a grin that reminded me of the taxi driver in Ankara, he could fix the car. Unfortunately, it was late, he and his assistant were tired and their wives expected them home for supper. He'd work on the car tomorrow. Tania seemed more put out than me about the delay. She seemed in a hell of a hurry to visit relatives and find roots that might not even exist.

Once in the sparsely furnished room above the tavern, though, she relaxed and accepted the inevitable. We had to delay our trip to Hopa and our try at the Russian border. We had dinner in the dingy tavern dining room and went to our room. To my surprise, Tania rummaged through her suitcase and brought out a fancy first aid kit. She removed the bandage from my shoulder, gagged at the sight of the ugly, jagged wound, then set about replacing the bandage with a clean one.

When we made love, she was totally relaxed, as though we were lovers on a Black Sea vacation.

Even so, I detected a subtle but definite change in her. Ever since that moment in the car when she'd seemed to have come to some decision, she'd been different. Quieter, more pensive. And her eyes, when she gazed into mine, had more sadness in them than fear. And yet the fear was there. I'd seen that kind of look in the eyes of people who had a loved one about to die of cancer or some other horrible disease. What did she know? What had she decided? What had her mind discovered about me?

The next morning, when we'd finished breakfast, the mechanic came into the dining room.

"Hey, 'merican man, car all fix up. Sound like new. You come see-listen."

He was right. The engine purred like a ferocious cat eager to spring on a choice prey. The mechanic beamed like a new father as we walked around the car and marveled at its performance. I offered the pleased mechanic another twenty dollars, but he wouldn't take it.

"Already overpay, 'merican. Most time, charge ten dollar. You pay forty. Muzbek just happy, happy make sick come well."

Ten minutes later, on the road to Hopa, I made a decision.

"Let's forget the fishing boat idea," I told Tania. "It's such an obvious way to get into Russia that the coast will be heavily guarded. Besides, once the fishing boat dropped us off, we'd have no way to get around."

"Whatever you say," she said. "You're the leader on this scouting expedition."

While we'd been waiting in Trabzon, I'd picked up a road map of Turkey. There was a direct route from Hopa to the border, but it ended there. The nearest highway into *Sovyetler Birligi*, as the map called the USSR, was out of Borcka, about thirty-five miles southeast of Hopa. The road went to Batum, just across the border, then wound its way up through the Caucasus. There were many roads on the Turkish side, precious few in that part of Russia. We'd be like two big fish in a very small fishbowl, clear water all around.

But the map did show a small road leading off the main highway to Batum, just this side of the border. I'd give that road a try.

We eased through Hopa with no trouble. On the highway to Borcka, the Chevrolet purred with such efficiency that I knew it would take us all the way to Moscow if there were no obstacles, such as roadblocks or armed soldiers, in the way.

Beyond Borcka, the road was broad and well kept, but not well traveled. We saw no cars at all. But not far from the border, we saw six big trucks coming the opposite way. They were empty, but I could tell by the smell and filth of the trucks that they carried fertilizer.

The Chevy continued to perform admirably. At one time, we actually got the relic up to sixty, moving along so fast and trouble-free that I missed the dirt road and had to backtrack. Once on it, I noticed that Tania's nerves were going taut. She began working her hands in her lap, licking her lips, looking with frightened eyes at the horizon.

We came through a narrow pass where they'd had to use dynamite to lay down even a dirt road. Tania fumbled in her purse, watched the tops of the rocky buttes on either side of the pass and drew out a small .32 caliber pistol.

"You're chock full of surprises," I said, pointing to the gun. "Can you use that thing?"

"I don't know. I've never fired a gun in my life."

I believed her. She held the gun between her thumb and forefinger, as though it were something she'd picked up from the carpet when there were plenty of dogs around. Gradually, she eased the pearl handle into her palm and tried her finger on the trigger.

"If you have to use it," I told her, hoping to get enough advice through to keep her from shooting herself—or me— "pull back on the hammer. That'll make it easier to pull the trigger. After the gun is fired once, the trigger will snap back on its own, ready for the next shot. Aim at what you want to hit and *squeeze* the trigger, don't *pull* it. Squeeze and don't anticipate the explosion of gunpowder. Just pretend it's your finger. Aim, squeeze, fire again. If you hit your first target, go on to the next one.''

"Target," she said hollowly. "You're talking about a man, a human being. Right?"

"In all likelihood. The rocks and trees in this barren place rarely attack unless rigorously provoked.''

She looked at me, digesting that, then burst out laughing. "Thanks, I needed that kind of straightening out. Still, I don't know if I can shoot at a human being.''

I shrugged. "If you can't," I said, "you can make book on the fact that the human being in question will blow you and your little popgun to kingdom come. Let's just hope we don't meet any humans who seem intent on stopping our progress.''

When I was certain that we were near the border, by checking the odometer and the mileage markers on the map, I pulled the old Chevy onto a patch of hard desert. Stunted growth grew in abundance, so it was easy to hide the car from any distant observation post and enemy binoculars.

"We cross after dark," I said. "For now, let's see if we can catch some zees. We'll be doing most of our travel by night.''

I don't know about Tania, but I slept like a mummy in the spacious back seat of the car. I awoke about ten thirty and Tania was sitting in the front seat, pulling back and lowering the hammer on the little revolver.

"Got the hang of it yet?" I asked.

She nearly leaped out of the car at the sound of my voice. I felt lucky that she didn't start shooting off that silly pistol. I apologized for startling her and got behind the wheel.

I drove with the lights off. Two miles farther, I saw the first observation post. The Turkish side. It was a rickety, old wooden tower about twenty feet high. A mile beyond was another post. Russian. It was also tottering and wooden, but was about thirty feet high. Both posts were dark. I entertained a faint hope that, because of budgets, neither post would be manned. I stopped the car, turned to Tania.

"This is the plan. I'm going to get this heap going as fast as I can and hope that neither side has dug any kind of ditch or put up a barrier. When we get close to the Turkish post, I'll hit the headlights. The Russians are most likely to have put something in the road, so we'll need the lights then. If there are no guards, we'll breeze through nifty as a knife."

"And if there *are* guards?"

I withdrew Wilhelmina and nestled the Luger between my thighs. I also slipped my pants down and took Pierre from his lambskin pouch. Tania watched all this with fascination.

"If there are guards and they fire at us," I said, "you'll see flickers of flame from their guns. Fire at those flickers. I'll be doing the same, left handed. If we get through without being mortally damaged, I'll drop this little present out the window as we pass the Russian post."

"What is it?"

"Poison gas."

There was a gasp and then a pause. "Tell me, Mr. Parson," Tania said at length, "just what government do you work for?"

"You ready?" I said, ignoring her question.

"As ready as I'll ever be."

But we never got the chance to put the plan into action. Apparently, the Turkish and Russian guards had become very chummy at this remote outpost. They were all on the Turkish side and they had been watching the Chevy come for some time.

As soon as I flicked on the headlights, we saw them. Eight of them, sneaking down the road toward us. Four Russian, four Turkish.

"Holy shit," I muttered. "We'll never get through now."

I shut off the lights, floored the accelerator and spun the wheel. The big car took off like a rocket, a whirling rocket. The rear tires, in a wild spin to the left, kicked up rocks and dirt. The front wheels hit the shallow ditch beside the road and then the hood seemed to be plowing through tough shrubs on the desertlike ground.

I heard booming sounds. From the corner of my eye, I saw the fiery flashes of automatic weapons being fired. At the same time, I heard slapping sounds as the bullets struck various parts of the big car.

And then came the pop, pop, pop of the little revolver. I

looked to my right; sure enough, Tania was hanging out the window, taking carefully aimed potshots at the guards. The firing stopped as the guards apparently hit the dirt for cover.

In that few seconds of time, bought for me by Tania's pearl-handled pistol, the Chevy hit the road again, heading west. In no time at all, we were beyond firing range.

But there'd be no border crossing tonight.

Maybe not ever.

Then I remembered the trucks I'd seen on the highway out of Borcka. They told me something about commerce between Turkey and Russia. And maybe a new way to crack the tight border security of the *Sovyetler Birligi*.

SIX

The company was called Murgul, after the small Turkish town where it was headquartered. I left Tania in the tavern room and went out there just after dawn. It was about twenty miles west of Borcka.

I went on a hunch. And that hunch was spawned from bits and pieces of information I'd picked up in my travels to various Eastern and Middle Eastern countries. It had to do with smuggling.

The company manager sat in a little cubbyhole office in a huge, sprawling wooden structure that smelled like the depths of the earth. Trucks from all over the eastern part of Turkey came to dump their special materials in the huge shed. The trucks marked Murgul hauled the stuff into Russia, which was badly in need of fertilizer.

As the pudgy manager looked up at me in his doorway, he spoke rapidly in Turkish. I spread my hands. There was a bunch of twenty dollar bills in them.

"Friend, I'm hoping you can speak even a little English," I said, grinning. "If not, maybe you recognize this green stuff."

"Speak English," he said with a grunt. "What for the money?"

I looked around to make sure we weren't overheard. Employees in heavy coveralls and masks worked in the big shed, mixing the fertilizer chemicals with the raw manure brought in from Turkish farms. They were all busy, some of them doing their jobs while still half asleep.

"My sister and I must get into Russia," I said. "We're willing to pay well. Can you sneak us in on one of your fertilizer trucks?"

He looked shocked, then grinned. He had amazingly white teeth and clear blue eyes. For a minute, I was afraid I'd stumbled onto an undercover KGB agent out to stop smuggling.

"You want to ride under a load of shit?"

"Not particularly," I said, then played my ace. "But if I have it figured right, you have special compartments in those trucks where a person or a parcel might be concealed from the Russians."

He sat back in his ancient, creaking chair. His face and hands were covered with a fine yellow dust. Fertilizer chemicals. And dried shit. He grinned, then frowned, then looked disgusted, then smiled. He got up, came around the desk. He took the twenties and stuffed them into a pocket.

"Where is sister?"

"At the tavern in Borcka. I can fetch her in an hour or less."

"Okay. Come see."

He led me through the shed and to an outside loading dock. There was a tall wooden structure, like a square silo. From it jutted a wooden chute, much like the ones Californians used to pan gold more than a hundred years ago. A stream of fertilizer was flowing down the chute into the back of an open truck. It could have been one of the six trucks I'd seen on the highway yesterday.

We went past the truck where several others sat empty. Drivers were in some of them, lined up to take loads from the spewing chute. The manager stopped at the last truck in line. The driver, knowing he had a long wait, was obviously off snoozing someplace.

With an agility that surprised me, the pudgy little man leaped onto the steel bed of the truck and motioned for me to follow. At the far end of the bed, near the cab, the manager stooped and lifted a steel panel. Below was a space large enough to hold two or three people, or a hell of a lot of contraband. At each end of the coffinlike cubicle were ventilators that could barely be seen from the outside of the truck.

"In here," the manager said, "you get shit down collar when truck hit bumps. Plenty bumps between here and Tiflis. If Russkies stop, we know nothing. You say you throw away tools and climb in here all by selves, hokay?"

"Yes."

"Cost you six more of these greeneries."

I'd already given the guy three hundred dollars, now he wanted a hundred and twenty more. What the hell, it was Hawk's money, and the guy was taking a hell of a risk. And asking no questions, even though he knew my story was a lie. I gave him eight more twenties to assure ourselves of a happy transporter.

"One thing," I said. "Is there a way out of that hole when the truck is loaded?"

"You don't want to go to Tiflis?"

"Not particularly. Mostly, we don't want to climb out when there are people around."

"No having problem. Driver dump load in Tiflis, drive from city on returning trip, stop in country, open hole and you popping out. Hokay?"

"Okay." I didn't like that plan at all, but it was the best I could do. And I'd sized up those vents, knew that, if worse came to worse, I could kick one out and squeeze through the hole while the truck was running. It was nice to know that, just in case.

"Come back one hour," the squat little man said. "I hold up load for one hour only. If late, driver come piss off and I got to make pay with greeneries. If late, owe more greeneries for driver."

I nodded and took off in the Chevy, which was still purring along so sweetly that I couldn't believe my good fortune.

Even over the bumpy roads, I was at the tavern in twenty-five minutes. I paid our bill and skittered up to the room.

"We're all set," I called out as I opened the door and rushed inside. "We'll be a little cramped and we'll smell crap all the way, but. . ."

The bathroom door was closed, and I'd thought Tania was in there. Even as I talked, I had the sinking sensation that the room and the bathroom were both empty. I opened the bathroom door. Nothing.

"Tania?"

I ran back downstairs, but the desk clerk couldn't understand English. I made a woman's shape with my hands and he grinned with yellow-toothed understanding. He pointed off down the street.

"Where? Where down the street did she go?"

He shrugged and made a gesture with his hands; it was the gesture of a person disappearing.

Just to make sure Tania wasn't still in the tavern, I searched the bar and the sleazy dining room, checked the restroom (they didn't have separate ones for men and women) and went back upstairs again. She was gone.

I got in the car and drove slowly down the street. I zigzagged around the area. After a few blocks, I was at the market area where cars weren't allowed. I decided to take one more look at the tavern, then to begin tearing this town apart looking for Tania. I parked, leaped out and ran into the tavern.

The manager of the tavern was behind the desk. He and the clerk were conversing loudly in Turkish, gesturing as though threatening each other with bodily harm. The manager saw me and smiled.

"Ah, Mr. Parson. So sorry miss you. Being in other part when you come for lady. She go away, leave you this."

He handed me a small pink envelope. I ripped it open. A note from Tania was inside:

Thanks for getting me this far. I can make it on my own now. If you also make it, perhaps we'll see each other in the Rostov area, if you should happen to be in the neighborhood. Bye, bye, Mr. Parson. You are good.

Shit!

That was the only word that came to mind. And I would be riding under a few tons of it very soon. But I missed Tania. Even though she was an extra burden, she was great company, and the way she'd handled that pistol the night before, gave me new respect for her.

And, I had to admit, there was a special feeling for her and the way she was in bed. I would miss her terribly, but I had no time now to dwell on the subject.

I had less than twenty minutes to get back to that fertilizer factory.

Naturally, I was late. Forty dollars' worth. The pudgy manager threw in a pair of clean overalls, a scarf and a mask to keep the shit from my body, neck and lungs. I crawled into the "tool" space and the driver dropped the steel slab in place. Light came from around the panel and through the vents at my head and feet. But not for long.

The truck cranked up, moved forward, and the space around me was soon filled with foul-smelling dust that turned the whole world black. Even with the mask, I thought I'd suffocate. Worse, the smell was threatening to make me vomit. I kept swallowing, swallowing, and the bile stayed down.

After what seemed an eternity, the truck began to move, hitting every bump the driver could find. Long before we were on smooth pavement, the cubbyhole where I lay fighting back the act of vomiting was almost full of fertilizer that had showered down through the cracks around the panel.

The trip seemed interminable. For the most part, the big truck rumbled along at a fair pace, hitting only an occasional bump. At intervals, it slowed and stopped as the caravan of trucks moved through a town. And then it stopped for a very long time and I could hear Russian voices coming through the vents. I felt the truck shift after voices had moved near and I knew that men had crawled on top of the fertilizer. I heard muffled sounds from back in the bed, like steel hitting steel through a wad of cotton.

The men on top were spearing long poles down through the dusty fertilizer, probing for contraband or people. Either it hadn't occurred to the Russians to remove the side vents and peer into the so-called tool space, or they'd been paid to leave that space alone. All their probing and holding up the Turkish drivers was part of the game.

Soon, the men leaped off the truck and we rumbled forward. I knew then that I was finally back in Russia. This time, though, my name was known, thanks to a crazy American going about the country killing political officers and leaving my name in his wake.

The last kill, according to Hawk, had been made near the small city of Lugansk, north of the seacoast city of Rostov. Rostov. Christ, that was the town Tania had mentioned in her note. I could have sworn that she'd told me she was heading for the Kharkov region where her father's family lived. Kharkov was an inland Ukraine city, at least two hundred miles north of Rostov.

Okay. It still fit. The family could be spread between Rostov and Kharkov. But why had she said Kharkov first and then mentioned Rostov in her note? To throw me off? Possibly, but why?

A picture began to form in my mind. I didn't like the way it was shaping up, so I mentally erased it. I finally fell asleep, lulled by the swaying of the truck—even over the Russian roads that were twice as bumpy as the Turkish ones.

I awoke to a feeling of rising. That was different. I was usually falling in my dreams. But this wasn't a dream. I heard the strange, high-pitched motor and knew that the truck was a dump truck. The bed was being raised and me with it.

Suddenly, there was a shuffling sound, then a great whooshing as the fertilizer slid off the truck. The driver inched forward, working the motor controls to bump the bed up and down. And then the truckbed began to lower, the truck to pick up speed. After a few more stops, where Russian voices blended with Turkish, the truck was moving fast again.

I shook the dusty fertilizer off my back and tried to push up the steel panel. The driver must have locked it, or it was too heavy for me. I waited. A half hour later, the truck stopped and I heard the driver open and close his door, heard crunching footfalls outside.

Boots rattled in the empty truckbed and then the panel was raised. The driver grinned down at me, a padlock in his hand; he'd locked the damned thing to keep me from emerging prematurely. At least, I preferred to think that was the reason for locking the panel.

I stood up in the truckbed and saw that we were in open country. There wasn't even a farmhouse or barn in sight. But three cows lazed in a nearby meadow, so I knew that humans weren't far away. I shook off the stinking fertilizer, exercising my arms and legs to get rid of the wobbles. When I jumped off the truck, my knees gave out and I fell smack on my face. The driver laughed idiotically, got into his cab and drove away.

My watch said one-fifteen. That was about right, considering the position of the hot sun. I calculated which was northwest and, ignoring the road, set off across the fields. Not far beyond the cows was a large haystack, eaten out around the base as though huge mice had been at work on it. I figured to get to the haystack, take off the grimy overalls, as well as all my clothes, shake off the fertilizer that had turned to paste with my sweat, then continue on. With luck, there would be a pond beyond the haystack and I'd take a much needed bath.

There was no pond.

There were three Russian farmers with pitchforks. They'd seen me climb off the fertilizer truck and were waiting for me.

My choices were few as the Russians advanced on me with their old-fashioned but very lethal weapons. I could shoot all three, hide them in the haystack and hope they weren't discovered before I was far from this place. Or I could run.

After several hours in that cramped tool space, I doubted my ability to run well, or fast, or far. But I had to try. These people were innocent patriots who'd seen an alien enter their land. I knew a bit of Russian, but not the Caucasian dialect, so I didn't dare open my mouth.

But I could get in a little practice before demanding that my body start running.

As the farmers approached, I singled out the smallest of them and made my lunge. With a well-placed karate kick, I sent his pitchfork flying through the air. He let out a yell and backed off. The biggest of the three also yelled, but not in fear. He roared at me, his pitchfork at belt level.

I sidestepped the lethal weapon, grabbed it in my left hand and slammed my right fist into the man's face. I gave it all I had and it was apparently enough. The man fell like a rock from the sky. I wheeled around to the third man and he was deliberating whether to attack or run. I made a jump toward him, growled deep in my throat and the deliberation was over.

He ran. Right behind him was the small guy whose pitch-fork I'd kicked helter-skelter. The third man was coming to. I clocked him once more and, as he was settling back against the haystack, I took off running, heading west in the general direction of the Black Sea.

My running legs held up for only ten minutes, but it was enough to get me off that farm. I walked fast for another twenty minutes, then slowed to a leisurely pace. I could see houses and barns here and there, but I avoided them.

As afternoon began to close out and my hunger built, I began to wish that I'd brought food along. Then again, I doubted that I'd want to eat anything that had been in that foul space with me and all that showering fertilizer. And I needed more than food and a bath. I needed wheels. It wouldn't take long for the three farmers to report to their local political officer, even less time for him to summon the police and then the local contingent of the KGB.

I was, I knew, a small metal duck moving across a very large shooting gallery.

Just before nightfall, I came to a long, wide irrigation ditch. The water looked pretty foul, but it was better than the itching grime that stuck to my body. I shucked all my clothes and, careful not to get my shoulder bandage wet, I waded in and took a bath. I even waded upstream and drank some of the water. Surprisingly, it tasted clean and good.

After drying, shaking out my clothes and getting dressed again, I decided that the ditch might have another purpose. I'd been running and walking across relatively flat ground. If authorities were looking for me, a pair of binoculars from a distant road could track me for miles.

Since the irrigation ditch ran generally north and south, I followed it until the water became shallow. I waded in ankle-deep water and then was in mud, then on dry ground. Eventually, I knew, the ditch would lead me to a stream or to a farm. And then I figured it out. The ditch ran downhill and I was now heading uphill. The water was deep where I'd found the ditch because it was close to the farms it served. If there'd been scant rainfall this spring, the stream that fed this ditch wouldn't be doing any feeding right now. With that kind of reasoning, I was certain that I was headed toward the water's source—a river or a creek.

I was right. But there were a number of farms and communes along the way. I kept low in the ditch and just kept on moving. At a small independent farm, I saw an orchard. The apples on most of the trees were small, hard and green. One section of the orchard had a few trees with huge, ripe yellow apples.

With one eye on the distant farm and barn and the other on the apples, I climbed out, collected a dozen apples, stuck them in my pockets and returned to the ditch. I sat on the bank and ate one, then two, of the apples. My stomach rumbled with approval, but I knew that one more apple might send it into rage.

I moved on. Darkness fell. Fatigue came like a shroud over all my being. I found a flock of haystacks at another farm, crawled into one of them and settled in for a long night of sleep.

Sleep wouldn't come. I kept thinking about Tania, missing her, wondering why she'd taken off on her own. Or had she been captured by the KGB men who'd spotted us at the airport in Ankara? Anything was possible.

And yet, thoughts kept niggling at me.

I really believed her story about her father's relatives in Russia, but I had serious doubts that she'd go through all this trouble just to visit them, see what they were like. We both could have been killed at the airport in Ankara and again at the border. Then again, once she got inside to visit her relatives, how did she expect to get back out again?

I recalled something Hawk had said about the killer, the American using my name, having set up an access route through Cyprus. The Russians had discovered his method of entering and leaving the country and had dispatched agents to Cyprus to catch him. They'd missed him, but had gotten onto my trail since I happened to be in Cyprus.

That meant that the Cyprus route was closed to the man who called himself Nick Carter. He had to find a new one.

I had set out to find a route into Russia and had run into

Tania. Or, to be more explicit, she had run into me. Deliberately. Why?

Another thing. Tania hadn't been nabbed by the KGB while she waited for me in the tavern room in Borcka. She'd left a note indicating that she'd left of her own free will. Of course, the KGB could have forced her to write that note. But she'd said she might meet me in Rostov when all along she'd said her destination was Kharkov.

And the photo taken by the KGB man—the grainy one of the khaki-clad man in the barn loft—had been taken at a farm just north of Rostov.

I finally slept there in that soft, sweet-smelling haystack. But it was an uneasy sleep.

I knew for certain now that Tania Koselke was somehow tied to the man who was killing the commissars. She was either coming to aid him, or to establish a new entry/exit route, or. . .

The zees caught up with me and I entered a different kingdom of nightmares.

SEVEN

I ran out of apples at noon the following day. My stomach went into rage.

By mid-afternoon, I found the small river that was supposed to be feeding the irrigation ditch. The water was low, but I drank from its muddy supply anyway.

If I swung left, I knew I'd eventually come to the Black Sea. If the KGB didn't get me, that is. I knew that I was a hunted man by now. Those farmers back near Tiflis must certainly have reported me; they'd be crazy not to.

I was just deciding to set out across the river and keep on a northerly heading when I saw the railroad bridge about a mile to my right. I went there and, sure enough, the tracks were shiny as though they were in frequent use.

Along about dusk, when my stomach was giving me all kinds of hell for ignoring it so long, a slow freight came chugging across the rolling desertlike land. I waited in brush alongside the railway embankment until the engine had gone past. I dashed out, ran as fast as I could, reached out for the iron grips at the end of an open flatcar, missed and tumbled headlong into the harsh gravel. Pain like a fiery finger ripped through my shoulder.

I allowed myself only a few seconds of self-pity. The train was still rumbling along, faster than I'd first thought. I got up, forced my legs to run again. This time, I caught the safety rings of an open boxcar, climbed to the roof, skittered along to the center and swung down into the open doorway.

The car was empty. The rough board floor offered no soft haven, but was better than a Russian prison. I curled up in a corner where the wind wasn't quite so strong and tried to get some rest. This walking and running and catching freight trains and eating apples and drinking filthy water was beginning to take a toll.

As hard and splintery as the floor was, it was a welcome change from my previous mode of travel. I slept, off and on, for several hours. Shortly before dawn, the train began to slow, then it stopped. I crawled to the door, looked left toward the caboose, saw nothing but a lot of Russia stretching off into the predawn glow.

To the right were lights and a high wooden tower that was a dispatcher's station. I saw men moving about with rifles and knew that they weren't railroad workers coming down to check the commodities on this train. They were local police or, more likely, KGB.

I slipped out of the train and took to the fields again. A small wooded area stretched out before me and I made for it, hoping to reach it before full dawn broke. The woods were thick. I dashed into the trees, made a right turn and followed the line of the tracks. After I'd gone what I figured to be two miles, I hit off to the right again. I came out of the woods only a hundred yards from the tracks and well beyond the dispatcher's tower. To my left, far, far away, I could see the tops of what I estimated to be fairly high buildings. It could be Rostov, but even if it were, it was still a good ten miles away. I had no stomach for walking the distance.

I waited in a clump of bushes near the track and, sure enough, here came the train, chugging slowly after its check stop at the dispatcher's tower. I could only hope that the KGB guys had checked it out good, concluded that I was still far south of this point and wasn't pulling a fast one on them.

My heart was pounding with fear, though, when I made another dash for the boxcar with the open door. This time, the train was moving much slower, so I caught up with the open doorway and heaved myself part way in, ready to drop back again if there were guards inside. It was empty, so I pushed hard and slid across the splintery floor. For my efforts, I got a rash of splinters in both hands and one big one down around my thigh.

I sat in a corner and picked out the splinters and wondered how long it would take them to get infected, to fester, and for the infection to reach my heart and stop it cold.

Knock it off, Carter, I told myself. You didn't come all this way to start feeling sorry for yourself, to let your mind peddle gloom and doom to your body.

There would be another check and search before the train entered Rostov, so I knew I'd have to pick a place to leave the train. I gazed out at farmland, searching for remote haystacks. And orchards.

The train engineer cut loose with his whistle and I snapped my head to the right. Up ahead was a collection of low buildings near the tracks. A railroad station or storage depot. The train was moving at a good clip now.

And then I saw a single guard standing in the center of the tracks. He looked like a tiny speck up there, but I could see enough to tell that he had a rifle raised above his head. He was there to halt the train at an unscheduled stop. Christ, they were going to search the empty cars again. The whistle kicked off again and then the train began to slow.

I couldn't wait for it to slow enough to make my jump a safe one. We were getting too close to that man with the rifle. I could make him out pretty good now.

The tracks made a little lurch to the left and I lost sight of the man with the upraised rifle.

In that moment, I leaped.

I rolled my body in the time-honored manner of the hobo and struck the steep embankment with my shoulders. I rolled like a badly spun frisbee and slammed into a wooden fence at the bottom of the embankment. For the next twenty seconds, I didn't know whether I'd broken my entire body or just most of it.

As it turned out, I hadn't broken anything. I had opened my shoulder wound, though. And there were enough bruises in my various muscles to start them to complaining along with my stomach. And thirst was getting to me. My last drink had been hours ago in that dirty river.

The train had already rumbled past and stopped for the guard (or guards) up ahead by the time I got myself untangled from the fence. Though I was certain I couldn't be seen down there, I crawled through brush until I was in another small woods. I got up, knelt behind a tree and looked back at the train. The crewmen were outside talking to three armed guards while another guard was walking alongside the train, peering atop flatcars and inside boxcars. I could see the legs of yet another guard on the opposite side of the train.

I headed off westerly again, figuring to reach the Black Sea and to enter Rostov from the coast. Once in Rostov, I knew, I'd have to play it cool until I found and befriended an English-speaking tourist. Hopefully an American. The lovely seacoast town wasn't exactly full of tourists, but it did draw some hearty, adventurous souls who didn't mind being well behind the Iron Curtain—and doing without certain luxuries that are so common and taken for granted in the West.

I desperately needed to find someone who was bilingual in English and Russian. Only then could I even keep track of where the commissar-killer had struck. My knowledge of spoken Russian was minimal; my reading and writing of it was worse.

Anyway, that was my plan. I also hoped to learn if a lovely young American girl had made her presence known yet. A tourist would know that—especially one of the jetsetters.

At the western edge of the woods, I peered out, hoping to see the waters of the Black Sea. What I saw was another farm. A really nice one, this time. The house was big and well cared for. There was an enormous barn, recently painted. Beside it was a low shed, open at both ends. Inside the shed was a huge farm wagon with high wooden sides. There were a number of small white outbuildings housing sheep, pigs and goats. The barn, I surmised, held a number of cows and horses. And there was a chickenhouse. All this attested to the farmer's prosperity. Most American farms could put this place to shame, but in Russia—especially in the Caucasus and the Ukraine—it was a model of prosperity and well-being.

As I watched, drinking in the sights of the pretty farm and wondering if there was any ready food for humans in the many outbuildings, a girl came down the back steps of the farmhouse with a large wicker basket. Even from that distance, I could tell that she was attractive.

The girl wore a pink, billowing skirt and walked as though

there were cushions of air under her feet. I was accustomed to seeing farm girls plod along like dray horses, toting their heavy loads, bowing from the burden, that kind of stuff. Not this girl. She fairly danced across the wide barnyard and went inside the barn.

I waited a few minutes for her to come out, figuring she'd gone in to deliver or pick up something. When she didn't emerge, I left the woods, ran a hundred quick yards across a newly plowed field, keeping the barn between me and the farmhouse. I crouched, waiting, watching the door the girl had used. Nothing.

When I reached the side of the barn, after crossing a fence and ripping my trousers on one of the pickets, I flattened myself against the wall. I put my ear to the boards, but heard nothing from inside. I eased along to the corner and saw that I couldn't go in the same door the girl had used without being seen by someone from the house. I went the other way and around that corner were a number of doors.

The first door led to a narrow stall with a small opening at the other end. A chicken hatchery, from the smell and look of it. The second door led to a stall where a large horse gazed dumbly at me. The third door led to the main barn chamber and I quickly darted inside.

It took a few minutes for my eyes to get used to the gloom. I made out other stalls, several feed bins, more horses and cows, some tools and a ladder to the loft. I was just ready to open one of the bins when I heard a sound from the loft. Someone moving about in hay or straw. I waited, expecting to see the girl with the light-footed walk come down the ladder, her pink skirt billowing. The thought intrigued me, but I'd more likely see a crusty old farmer with a pitchfork and no tolerance for strangers.

The sound from upstairs died. Still, I waited. My curiosity soon nagged me and I went to the ladder. I climbed as silently as I could, but the old boards creaked and groaned under my weight.

When I reached the top, there was a matting of straw about two feet thick. From beyond it somewhere, bright light streamed into the barn. I inched up a bit more on the ladder and saw the girl.

She was sitting in the open loft door, the wicker basket

beside her. Her legs were dangling over the side of the doorway and she was reaching into the basket for something. She brought it out and my mouth and stomach went wild. It was a huge drumstick.

I inched up more and stared out the window past the girl. I'd been right about being close to the Black Sea. Three hundred yards beyond was a roadway. Beyond that was a row of lovely summer cottages. Next came the shimmering surface of water. A great deal of water. Far out, I could see a few sailboats. Beyond them was a freighter chugging to the north.

"Well, are you coming up or do you just want to hang there?"

The girl's voice—silky-smooth and speaking perfect English—startled me so much that I lost my grip on the ladder. I slipped down three rungs before I snatched hold of a rung and held on. By then, the girl was standing above me, smiling, licking chicken off her fingers.

She laughed, then motioned for me to come up.

"You must be the famous Nick Carter," she said as I eased onto the straw of the loft. "I have made fantasies about you coming to see me, but I never really expected to see you. You *are* Nick Carter, aren't you?"

It was all too much.

I mean, the mind and the body and the stomach can take just so much punishment. The world went black while I stood there. I don't even remember hitting the straw.

I do remember waking up, still in the loft, with the girl tending to me. She'd gone down for water, bandages and medicines. My lips were wet with water she'd tried to get down my throat. A wet cloth was folded across my forehead. And she'd removed my shirt and was replacing the blood-soaked bandage on my shoulder.

"Those things answer my question," she said, pointing to Wilhelmina and Hugo. "You are Nick Carter. But where did you hide your high-powered rifle?"

And then I knew. She thought I was the crazy assassin who was using my name. And yet she was helping me, wasn't even afraid of me. I was curious about that, but even more curious about the food and the water situation.

"Can we talk about that later?" I asked. "I've had nothing

but a few apples the past two days, and drank only from an irrigation ditch and a scrawny river. I think I'm about to starve."

She laughed. Unlike Tania's laugh, this girl's was delicate, tinkling, full of fun. And she was as slender as a whip. When I tried to sit up, I found that those slender arms had a great deal of strength. She pushed me back and went to work taping the new bandage in place.

"You have been sorely abused," she said in textbook English, "and I really should have Mr. Schamkin look at your shoulder. He's a veterinarian. But I've helped him fix up animals, so I suppose you will be all right. As for starving or dying of thirst, I think you're not in great danger there. Wait until I patch you up, then you can eat and drink."

When the bandage was done and she'd helped me into my shirt and jacket, she brought the basket over. She gave me a sip of sweet cider, then a cracker with cheese on it.

"We mustn't sit by the open door," she said, like a clucking mother hen. "And you mustn't gulp a lot of food and drink. Take it slowly. Then, you can tell me all about yourself and what you've been doing to those—"

She bit off her words, but I could tell from her blazing eyes that the words would have been vitriolic. I munched and sipped, much to the displeasure of my stomach that was telling me to gulp and be ravenous.

"I always eat my suppers out here," she said, turning to gaze fondly through the window at the distant sea. "That is, since I've been home on vacation. It's so peaceful up here and I can make the fantasies about so many things. Tell me, what is just beyond the sea? Right over there?"

She was pointing in the general direction of Poland, but I didn't want to tell her that. This girl obviously had freedom on the brain.

"Turkey," I said. "I'd say Istanbul is not far from the end of that long and lovely finger."

She smiled, laughed, then blushed. "You have a lovely way of saying things, Mr. Carter. It is hard to believe. . ."

Again, she cut off her words. I didn't probe, not yet. I had graduated to a chicken breast and I was cheating a bit, nipping when she was looking, chomping when she wasn't.

And I was on my third cup of cider.

"You mentioned being home on vacation," I said. "You can't be more than sixteen or seventeen. Are you on vacation from school?"

"In a way," she said. "But I graduated a year ago and am now a full member."

"Member of what?" I was certain she was going to say the Communist Party and it would be all over for me.

"The Bolshoi Ballet," she said. There wasn't the pride in her voice that should have been there.

"That's quite an accomplishment," I said. "You should be proud." I remembered my first sight of her, how she'd seemed to sail across the ground without touching it.

"I am proud," she said. "I am just not free."

I sighed. "And what do you know of freedom?"

She looked straight at me, challenging. Her eyes, I noticed, were bright green and very pretty.

"Enough to know that I want it. Ever since Danielle brought me those forbidden books, I've been dying to be free."

I looked around the place, remembering the well-kept buildings of the farm, the obvious look of money about the place. "It seems to me," I said, "that you have about all the freedom you could ask for. You're a member of the Bolshoi. Your parents have this great farm and—"

"Don't be ridiculous," she said. "This is what you call in America a 'perk.' It is my annual prize for doing all that is required of me. The money that I should be paid goes to keep this farm in good order. The people who own it, Boris and Marisa Schamkin, are kind of surrogate parents. They are nice to me, but I feel that they are nice only because of the money the government gives them. I spend all my holidays here. And my annual vacation."

"Where are your parents?"

She looked at me gravely. "I don't know. They were very poor, from up north somewhere. I was taken from them when I was three years old, when I showed an ability for the ballet. I have been in training ever since. I have been given the name Ilena Boritsky. I don't know what my real name is."

It suddenly began to sound like a dismal way to live. I

changed the subject. "What books did you read—the ones that made you yearn for freedom?"

Her animation was back. She knelt beside me, her eyes wide and glistening. "Oh, they were marvelous books. *The Adventures of Tom Sawyer*, *Gone With the Wind*, *The Hobbit* and *The Lord of the Rings* trilogy, *Portnoy's Complaint*, *Catcher in the Rye*, *The World According to Garp*, *Bullet Park*—and, oh so many more that are forbidden. And now," she said, riveting me with those green eyes, "you must tell me about you. Tell me about your wonderful exploits."

"First," I said, "tell me why you think this Nick Carter is such a hero. After all, the whole Russian government is after him for killing their political officers."

She made a face and looked every bit like an American teenager, wrinkling her nose at a bad joke. "They are criminals and murderers also. You are doing right to eliminate them."

"You think so, Ilena? What do you know of them? What have they done?"

She looked surprised, even a little shocked, as though I should know the answers to those questions.

"Why, everyone in the region knows what those commissars have been doing. They are common thieves and rapists and murderers. They take what they want from the people, the young daughters—even the young boys, I have heard. They take farms and animals as if they were their very own. And if someone complains to the police, that someone disappears. You, Mr. Nick Carter, have become that wonderful man from England who stole from the rich and gave to the poor."

"Robin Hood?"

"Yes, Robin Hood. I have not read his book, but I shall someday, when I get to America. There is much talk about him, in certain circles."

"You're a very brave and lovely girl, Ilena," I said. "I hope you get your wish. But tell me, do others feel the way you feel about this Nick Carter?"

"Oh, of course. Everyone knows what certain commissars have been doing. Oh, I don't mean all of them. Just those in this region. They have become despots, evil, overbearing, cruel murderers and thieves. The people secretly help you. You should know that. If people didn't help you, the way I'm helping you, you would have been caught and imprisoned long ago. Or killed."

I chewed on that a bit. I was full of chicken, crackers, fruit and cheese, and my stomach literally gurgled from the twelve cups of cider I'd drunk.

"What about government reaction?" I asked. "The officials certainly don't look on this Nick Carter as a Robin Hood."

"Oh my no. The newspapers and radio constantly brand him a spy from the American government. They say he has come to destroy the beauty that is communism. TASS says that America wants war and that the killer spy has been sent here to provoke us into that war."

I didn't see how one man killing a few political officers in one region of Russia could lead to an all-out war, but then I had to consider Soviet logic. The important thing was that this girl was helping me; others would help if I played my cards right.

For one thing, I didn't dare tell this girl that the man who'd been killing the commissars was using my name and that I had come to stop him. For another, if I assumed the passive role of this fake Nick Carter, he'd soon enough get word of it and might even come gunning for me. But I couldn't set up that kind of meeting here, in this girl's barn. The phony Nick Carter, whoever he was, wouldn't go down without a battle.

And the battle I envisioned would pretty much mess up this wonderful perk the Soviet government had provided for Ilena Boritsky. I decided then on a plan.

"Ilena, as you can tell, I'm not in shape to do much for the next few days. I can't tell you what happened, so please don't ask, but I need your help."

"Oh, anything," she gushed. "Anything at all."

"Would it be safe for me to hide out in this loft? Would you bring me food?"

"It would be safe. Boris has a bad leg and hardly ever comes up here. And Marisa, his wife and my surrogate mother, is too fat. She'd break the ladder if she tried."

Ilena was bubbling with impish enthusiasm now. One of her fantasies was coming true.

"Two nights should do it," I said, although I hated to waste the time. If the killer did a piece of work during that time, my new cover would be blown. Strange, I thought, it was the first time in my long career as Killmaster for AXE that I'd had to use my own name as cover.

"All right," Ilena said, gazing at me with a speculative look. "And, in exchange, you must do something for me."

"Name it."

"When you have finished killing all the bad commissars, you must take me with you to America. You must promise," Ilena said, her green eyes staring at me intently. "If you don't, then I will have to call the authorities and tell them you are here."

I doubted that she would do that; it would ruin a good fantasy. But I promised.

"When I leave," I said, sighing heavily, tiredly, "I'll take you with me."

She squealed so loud that I thought she'd pierced my eardrums. She slammed into my arms and hugged me with strong, ballet-toned muscles. The kisses from her wide, full lips were turning me on.

"Oh," she said, "I am so happy that you were wounded and had to come to me. I will care for you. I will make you well. And, when we go to America, I will make you a wonderful wife."

EIGHT

Boris and Marisa Schamkin didn't look at Nick Carter as a Robin Hood, as did other Soviet farmers in the region, according to Ilena. They were protected from crooked commissars by the fact that Ilena had full government protection. They thought of the man who was killing the commissars as a common crook, an enemy of the state.

But I saw the Schamkins each morning and each night. Boris, stocky and strong-looking, with an enormous black mustache, came limping out at dawn to feed the animals. Shortly afterward, Marisa, incredibly fat but with a sweet-looking face, would waddle out with two gleaming steel pails to milk her cows. Later, Boris would load up the enormous wagon with various items—mostly hay or straw, sometimes fertilizer—and ramble off down the main road to Rostov. His two great horses seemed to pull the huge wagon with no effort. The Schamkins didn't look dangerous, not at all.

In any event, Ilena kept coming, kept me well-supplied with food and chattered away like a magpie about all the wonderful things we'd do as man and wife in America. She asked, and I answered, somewhere in the neighborhood of nine million questions about life in America. And then she changed the subject, bringing out clippings she'd taken from the Rostov newspaper. The stories all involved the killing of various political officers in the Rostov-Kharkov area. Ilena read the clippings to me and, from them, I was able to compile a list, but unable to see a pattern in the actions of the phony Nick Carter.

Even though Ilena kept talking about us being man and wife, there was nothing of a sexual nature in her attentions to me. She kissed me frequently—great, wide-lipped, wet kisses on the mouth—but she never gave me an opening, and I never looked for one. It was a rousing but pure relationship.

On the second day, I'd made my plans and began to fire questions at Ilena. Where was the KGB headquarters in Rostov? How many other commissars were in the area? Did she know the names of any farmers north of Rostov, and around Kharkov, to whom I might go for help?

She gave me curious looks, as though I'd lost my mind and had forgotten things Nick Carter should know, but she answered as best she could. She got me a map and I began to find a pattern in the kills.

The American using my name had made only two kills south of Rostov. Most had been farther north, near Kharkov. And yet, Tania's note when she'd disappeared in Borcka had said maybe she'd see me in Rostov. I figured if she had anything to do with the killer that he was changing his base of operations.

The killings up around Kharkov had been completed, all the bad political officers weeded out. The assassin would be moving here for most of his action.

That evening, after Ilena had gone into the house, I decided to make my move. I'd told her I would stay the night and she said she'd pack me a basket of food, but I knew that would be a mistake. Boris and Marisa Schamkin had to be suspicious about her many trips to the barn loft and the long hours she spent there, not to mention all the food she was hauling out of the house.

Shortly past midnight, I crawled down from the loft, walked up and down the open space to get my legs functioning right, then slipped out the back door. I took off across the field, toward the woods.

It would be no good using the railroad. They were checking the trains closely. And hitchhiking was out. Hell, I couldn't even walk on the roads.

But, as I neared Rostov, farms became fewer, roads more

plentiful. Traffic was virtually non-existent because of the ten o'clock curfew. I saw a bus, a couple of trucks and a police car.

When I reached the first populated streets of outlying neighborhoods, I kept to back yards, hoping I wouldn't run across any sharp-eyed dogs. I had gone two dozen blocks through the residential section when I came to a broad intersection. Five streets met at the juncture. In the center was a small square and the inevitable statue of a soldier on a horse.

I checked the street names on the map Ilena had found for me. The one leading downtown and to the wharves was across the wide intersection, past the open square and the statue. There was no way to skirt around—I had to cross that wide space.

I made it to the statue with no trouble, but felt the hair rising on the back of my neck. I stood beside the statue and made a three hundred sixty degree turn. All the houses were dark, there was no traffic. The night was quiet and peaceful.

And then, up ahead, on the street leading downtown, a shadow moved.

For the next ten minutes, my eyes zeroed in on the area where something had moved. The shadow had moved only a little, as though someone had stepped onto the sidewalk and back against a fence.

I palmed Wilhelmina and attached her silencer. I ran a check on Hugo's muscle-spring release. Just by twitching certain muscles in my forearm, the razor-sharp stiletto released with a slithering sound and slid into my right hand. I checked to see that Pierre was in his lambskin pouch, replaced the stiletto in its sheath and, with my Luger in hand, I ran in a crouch across the intersection and slid into shadows alongside a small tavern.

From that vantage point, I surveyed the street again. Nothing. A bus rumbled past and I used its headlights to see if anything or anybody was hiding in the bushes along the house fences. Nothing.

With a shrug, and an admonition to myself to stop being so skittish, I began to walk down the wide street. I kept close to the fences, held Wilhelmina close to my hip and eyeballed both sides of the streets as I walked.

My footfalls echoed in the empty street, in the still night. I tried to walk easier, to float the way Ilena seemed to float, but I seemed only to make more noise. I was the plodding peasant girl, bowed by a heavy burden. My feet hit the pavement like hunks of lead.

An echo seemed to come from behind me, until I realized that it wasn't an echo at all. Someone else was walking on this sidewalk, and that someone was equally unable to keep his shoes from making noise in the quiet night. I stopped quickly.

There was a faint ka-lop sound, then silence. Someone was behind me and hadn't been able to stop when I did. I'd heard his extra footfall.

Sweat began to bead in my palms and forehead, to collect in my armpits. I walked on, thinking.

It couldn't be the police or the KGB. I was such an open, lonely target, they could have taken me at anytime. But it could be the killer I was seeking. If he and Tania were somehow tied, she would have warned him about me, and he would be waiting.

I decided it had to be the man who was killing the commissars. Somehow, he'd hit it lucky and had staked out the very street I was taking into the city. It figured. Only a man with considerable luck would be able to succeed at what he was doing.

I decided to keep walking and wait for him to make his move.

A block farther on, as I was crossing a street that seemed to divide the residential section from the business area, there was a shuffle of footsteps behind me as though someone had suddenly begun to run.

I was just turning when a voice rang out in Russian, commanding me to stop and put up my hands.

I did as ordered. But, when I started to raise my hands, my ears picked up movement from his nervous feet. I had him located. I whirled into a crouch and cut loose with Wilhelmina. I fired only twice, but once would have done the job.

The muffled cracks were hardly louder than ordinary footfalls on this dark, silent street. I saw a tall, slim figure in black. He was in the street, just beyond the curbing. He held a gun in his right hand, but the gun was already dangling loosely. The man was slowly falling to the pavement.

I ran to him, kicked the gun away and turned him on his back. A young man with blond hair and wide, frightened blue eyes looked up at me. There was a large splotch of blood on the chest of his black sweatshirt. I hadn't hit him in the heart, but I knew that the shot had been fatal.

"You bastard," the man said in Russian. "I almost had you."

"Yeah," I said in English. "If you get another chance to mug anybody, make sure it's a helpless old lady."

His eyes took on a curious glaze. "Mug?"

"Sure. Mug, rob, steal, hold up, whatever you call it here."

The man's face twisted in pain. He was closer to death than he realized.

"I am not a thief," he said, gasping out the words in slow motion. "I am . . . I . . ."

He died. No histrionics, no style. He just closed his eyes and died. His mouth was still open. I scanned the area, saw that no one had been alerted by the two muffled cracks of the silenced Luger and searched the young man who'd tried to take me.

Holy Jesus, I thought when I opened his wallet. Through all the Cyrillic symbols, I could make out his name and his title. He was assistant political officer for a region or county south of Rostov. His boss, the commissar, had been killed a week ago by the man calling himself Nick Carter. And here was the assistant, untrained in this kind of work, out to avenge the death.

The irony of it made me sad. This boy was looking for the phony Nick Carter, to kill him for having killed his boss, and had run smack into the real Nick Carter and had been gunned down for his efforts.

I was just about to drag his body out of the street when I saw a pair of approaching headlights. Another bus. I took off down the side street and heard the squeal of the bus's brakes. The driver had obviously spotted the dead man in black and was stopping. I didn't look back. I ran three blocks, turned right on a wide boulevard and came out at the wharves. All the buildings were dark. Some of them, I discovered, were empty.

I looked around, picked out a likely empty building, went around back and broke a pane of glass in the door. I unlocked the door and went in. On the third floor were bales of rags, baled for shipping. I pushed several of them onto a pile and made a nest for sleeping.

I'd had enough for tonight. I'd sleep and make plans for tomorrow.

Two hours later, I heard smashing and hammering from downstairs. Then voices raised in command.

Even though I barely had time to think of what to do next, one thought was clear: The body of the young assistant political officer I'd left on the street had been found and authorities were looking for his killer. What better place to look than empty buildings?

It sounded as though a whole platoon had come smashing into the building's first floor. I was on the third, so I had some small advantage. I found the stairs and went quietly to the fourth and top floor while those below continued to stumble about.

The top floor was empty. There was a trapdoor to the roof and a small ladder leading up to it. I tugged on the rungs to make sure they were safe. They were, but just barely. I climbed up, then stopped and cursed my foul luck.

There was a rusty old padlock holding the trapdoor shut.

And below me, the search party was already through with the first and second floors and were heading for the third where I'd slept in the bales of rags.

I took out Wilhelmina, attached the silencer, backed down a couple of rungs and took dead aim on the lock. It took two shots to break it. But even silenced reports cracked loudly in the big empty room.

As I was pushing up the trapdoor, I heard something directly below. I looked back. Two policemen were at the top of the stairs, panting, catching their breath. They had flashlights and I could almost *feel* the beam of one of them cross my body. The beam stopped and rose slowly to my face.

Both cops began to jabber in Russian. From the backlight

of flashlights below, I could barely make out their heads. As they started toward me, their flashlights homing in on me as I clung to that ladder, I took dead aim and shot the one on the right. The 9mm slug of hot lead barked and slapped its way through the silencer, through the shaft of light.

I saw blood and hair and brains fly away into darkness as the missile found its mark, squarely between the policeman's eyes.

The second cop broke and ran, heading back downstairs.

I opened the trap and went onto the roof. I quickly checked out the sides of the building and found a rusty old fire escape on one side. That was out. They'd pick me off halfway down. There was only a six-foot gap between the empty warehouse and the building; . either side and to the rear.

I decided on a rearward line of retreat, toward the sea. I leaped the six feet and landed on a roof that was so squishy I was surprised not to find myself tumbling down into the building. I ran like the wind, heading for yet another building.

I was just leaping to the next building, when I heard commotion behind me. I turned. Cops were streaming up through the trapdoor I'd used as my escape route. They didn't seem to know which way to go.

Taking advantage of their momentary confusion, I dropped to my knees and began to crawl. At least I wouldn't be silhouetted against the faint light coming from the harbor.

When I came to the next building ledge, I felt the flashlights searching for me. Fortunately, I was too far away, beyond the limits of those small hand-held lights.

Even so, I waited until the beams were flashing elsewhere before I raised over the ledge and calculated the distance to the next and last building on the block.

It was a big gap, perhaps ten or twelve feet. My body was already complaining about the sudden dash for freedom, and my right shoulder was giving me all sorts of pain.

I leaped.

In the darkness, I'd misjudged the distance. It was easily fifteen feet. I saw that I was going to miss clearing the ledge of the next building. In a fraction of a second, I saw the ground far below and imagined myself down there—dead.

My hands reached out, stretching, straining. As I came down, my hands slapped hard against the ledge of the next building. I curled my fingers like grappling hooks. My left hand caught on something solid, but my right hand had no such luck. The tile on the top of the ledge crumpled and pulled away in my right hand. Even as I struggled to gain better purchase, I heard the broken tile clatter and thump its way to the ground below.

I was hanging by my left hand, literally tearing the nails off my fingers, waiting to follow that tile into the blackness.

With an overhand swing, I brought my right arm up again, grabbed solid stone and began to pull myself up. I heaved my aching body over the ledge and lay for several seconds getting my breath back. The sounds of my pursuers came closer and closer.

I slid on my belly across the black, tarred roof, heading toward the side nearest the wharves. Halfway across, I found a small shed and a pair of chimneys. I stopped to contemplate the shed just as beams from nearby flashlights began to play along the roof.

Christ, the police had reached the final building and, unwilling to take the gamble I'd taken by leaping that great distance, they were lined up at the ledge looking for me with their flashlights.

I crawled behind the shed and chimneys, just as the lights played around the spot where I'd lain only seconds before.

I waited. If they saw the broken tile and convinced themselves that I'd made that incredible—though stupid—jump to the last building, they'd soon have a big plank brought up. They'd come after me.

I sneaked a look and saw the policemen—a dozen of them now—peering down the side of the building with their flashlights. They must have seen the broken tile down there. But the tile could have been knocked off by the wind. Even so, I couldn't count on the Russians' disbelief that I'd leaped to the final building in the block. I could count only on my own resources—and some luck.

Using the shed and the chimneys as a shield between me and the lingering, puzzled policemen, I crawled to the far edge of the building. There was a wide street below. Across, running for as far as I could see in either direction, were various-sized buildings, all of them one-storied. Between each building was a wooden walkway leading to a pier in the dark distance. Along each pier were dozens of fishing boats.

Far up to my right, toward the center of the city, were larger wharf buildings, longer piers, bigger boats. I saw a couple of full-sized freighters at two piers, and three more anchored in the harbor.

But it was the boats tied up at the nearest piers that caught my attention. They were all dark. Either they were empty or the crews were sound asleep. It was still three hours before dawn and, since the taverns were all closed or gone underground, it was a safe bet that the boat crews were snoozing away in their cozy little bunks.

And yet the boats seemed my safest haven, if there was a safe haven in this seaport city on the Black Sea.

I spotted a fire escape off to my right, but the beams of flashlights were still searching the roof of my building. The shed and chimneys were between me and the policemen, but I'd have to move out of their protection to reach the fire escape.

Then again, perhaps not.

I crawled over the ledge and, using my hands on the ledge—and hoping that another piece of tile wouldn't give way—dangled my body toward the street. Inching my hands along, I headed toward the fire escape.

I was only a few feet from it when two police vans came whizzing down the street alongside the wharf and squealed to a stop. I groaned and looked down.

A dozen cops came pouring out of the vans.

NINE

For some reason I didn't immediately understand, the policemen from the two vans didn't start throwing flashlight beams all over the building. They didn't even look up. I hung there, only a few feet from the fire escape, my fingers losing their grip on the slippery tiles.

But I could see the policemen moving about below. They were busy opening the rear doors of the vans.

And then I saw why.

From each van, the cops brought out long planks, like gangways used to board small ships or boats. The policemen back on the next building had apparently called for the planks so they could reach the building I was now on.

Why in hell, my mind asked, didn't they just come up the fire escape on this side?

Instead of cursing their stupidity, I counted my blessings. I inched closer to the fire escape and soon felt the hard steel beneath my feet. I crouched at the top of the rusty fire ladder, on a metal platform, and watched the proceedings below.

Ten of the cops went bustling up the side street, taking the huge planks to their buddies on the roof of the building behind me. But two cops remained, and they were walking toward the foot of the fire escape. They had flashlights and they played the beams over the steel gridwork of the fire escape.

They were coming up.

The Rostov police weren't nearly as stupid as I'd figured them to be.

My initial impulse was to wait for the two policemen to draw near, then to let Wilhelmina put them away. I hadn't come to Russia to start diminishing the population, only to get rid of one crazy American who was giving me a bad name.

But then I couldn't let these two policemen take me alive. There was just no way for me to escape the firing squad.

I looked around wildly, trying to think of some way to distract those two policemen. My eyes lit on a loose tile. I reached out to pluck it away from the building ledge, but it wouldn't budge.

Working swiftly, because the policemen had pulled down the straight ladder at the bottom of the fire escape and were almost to the second floor, I snapped Hugo into my hand and began to dig at the mortar with the sharp stiletto. I'd already resolved that if I couldn't get the tile loose and use it in some diversionary way, I would have to shoot the oncoming policemen. I couldn't drop Pierre on them. The gas would rise and take me along with them.

I worked Hugo swiftly and deftly under the tile, catching the loose mortar in my hands to keep it from clattering down through the metal steps and landings of the fire escape.

The cops were heading up to the third level.

I started counting under my breath. If the tile hadn't come loose by the count of three, I would put Wilhelmina to work.

One.

The two policemen paused at the third landing, shining their flashlights up through the gridwork and along the building ledge.

Two.

The first policeman started up to the fourth level while his partner surveyed adjacent buildings across the street. More mortar came loose, but the tile held firm.

Three.

I could hear two sets of footsteps on the fire escape, feel the old contraption sway with the weight of the oncoming policemen. I was ready to whisk the Luger from its snug holster, but decided to give one more tug on the tile.

It came loose.

Without hesitation, I flung the tile at a target I'd already picked out.

The hunk of tile arched through the dark Russian sky, sailed out over the narrow street between this building and the one on the opposite corner. The policemen were on the landing just below me. If I had reached down, I could have touched their caps.

Ka-plunk!

The tile hit the middle of the roof of the building across the street. The policemen stopped, stared that way.

"What was that?" one of them said in Russian.

"A noise. On the roof of that building," the other replied.

"Christ," the first man said. "We've got the wrong building. The killer-spy is over there."

Without even questioning their assessment of the situation, they retreated with foot-hammering swiftness down the rickety metal fire escape. I held onto the building ledge, just in case their crushing weight caused the fire escape to come loose from the building.

I watched the two policemen streak out into the dark street. One of them blew a whistle and called out in Russian that the killer was on the roof of the building across the street. I heard a flurry of footfalls, knew that other cops were running that way.

Slowly, quietly, cautiously, I descended the fire escape and ran noiselessly toward the center of town.

Two blocks later, I crossed the street and looked back to see a virtual sea of flashlight beams on the roof of the second building. The wrong building.

I didn't take time to compliment myself on a slick getaway, because I hadn't gotten away yet. I stood looking at the low wharf buildings, at the dark piers beyond. I selected one pier at random and ran between two small warehouses.

Fishing boats, and a few pleasure boats, were tied up on either side of the pier. I selected a battered, greasy-looking fishing boat that looked as though it might have been seaworthy in another century. It was a big one, at least eighty feet long, called the *Sonya*. I went up the gangway and stepped onto the slippery steel deck.

Quietly, I roamed over the boat. The crew's quarters were empty, as was the hold where fish had obviously been not too many hours before. Odors lingered in both places: one of old vodka, the other of dead fish. The crewmen had long since gone to their homes; the fish to market.

The captain's cabin, however, was another matter. I eased open the door and, sure enough, the captain was sound asleep in his bunk, snoring lightly. I stepped inside and closed the door.

An idea was forming in my brain, but I hadn't the slightest hope that it would work. Suppose this captain had also heard of Nick Carter and admired the man. Suppose, like Ilena, he had a yearning for freedom. The idea might be farfetched, then again . . .

I had to take the chance. In a matter of minutes, the police would figure out how I had eluded them and their search would widen. They'd most certainly include these dark and mostly empty fishing and pleasure boats in their search.

I went over to the captain's bunk and, palming Hugo just in case things went wrong, gently shook the man's shoulder. The captain opened his eyes groggily, saw me peering at him and awoke with a start. He let out a stream of Russian obscenities, then started to come up off the bunk. I let him see the stiletto and he fell back.

"Do you speak English?" I asked in my crude Russian.

"Of course," he said thickly, angrily. "Who are you?"

I swallowed hard and started in. "Have you ever heard of Nick Carter?"

"Ha," he roared. "Of course, sure, hearing of Nick Carter. He is man killing those crooked bastards. Bastards who are taking boats from good friends, perhaps coming now for my beautiful *Sonya*. Which are you, man with knife, Nick Carter or crooked commissar?"

I breathed easier. The idea might pay off. "Listen to me," I said, "and listen well."

I told him I was indeed Nick Carter, that the police were after me right now, but that the killing would end soon, hopefully in a matter of days. When the killing was done, I told him, I'd need a way across the Black Sea to Turkey for myself and a friend. For tonight, I said, I needed to be a member of his crew, perhaps even his first or second mate.

I gave him a few seconds to think all that over. Finally, he blurted: "Why killing end so soon? We got much more crooks in ranks of political officers."

"The killing will end," I said, "because they're getting too close to me. They almost got me tonight. Maybe someday I'll come back and finish the job, but now I have to think of escape."

He nodded.

"Am hearing in taverns that whole regiment of KGB coming here to catch you, Nick Carter. Sure, I lie to police if they come to beloved *Sonya*. As for later, going for Turkey, maybe perhaps not possible."

"Why not?"

"Only way out is through Strait of Kerch, between mainland and island of Krym."

I knew the area well. Krym Island, located in the northeastern sector of the Black Sea, formed the Sea of Azov, actually a large bay with Rostov at its northern point. Yalta, where the famed meeting between Roosevelt, Churchill and Stalin was held in the winter of 1945, was located on Krym. There was a narrow exit at the island's northern point, but there were rocks there to keep shipping at a minimum. The only logical way out of the Sea of Azov, I knew, was through the Strait of Kerch. The strait was narrow. Even high-powered rifles from the Caucasian mainland could pick us off.

But there was no other way. Even if I could steal a plane, we'd be shot down by Soviet MiGs before we were very far off the ground.

"Okay," I told the captain, whose name was Vasily Merkolov, "we'll worry about that later. Right now, my main concern is . . ."

I stopped when I heard heavy footfalls along the wooden pier.

"No good telling police you are crew member or first mate," Captain Merkolov said. "Put away knife. Showing you where to hide."

I'd still been holding the man on his bunk with Hugo's sharp tip at his throat. I resheathed the weapon and the captain tumbled out of his bed. He groaned from his beginning hangover, shook his head and then knelt on the floor.

At the side of his bunk was a slab of wood. The captain tapped one end of the board and then gave a sharp rap with the heel of his hand at the other. The board collapsed inward and he dragged it out. There was a dark space in there, perhaps three feet deep and only fourteen inches high, and as long as the bunk.

"Last captain keeping this hole full of vodka," he said, grinning at me in the darkness. "I using to bring back nice things am buying from Turk friends. Good for smuggling, good for hiding. Inside, quick."

I lay on my back and slid into the black space. I had the uneasy feeling that I was sliding into my own coffin, but I had no choice.

The captain replaced the board, tapping it in special ways to make certain the unusual locking mechanism received it properly. If the board weren't tapped first at one end and then rapped sharply at the other, in that sequence, the mechanism wouldn't let go. The only other way in was to use an axe. I just hoped the police didn't feel that strongly about what might lie beneath the captain's bunk.

The feeling of being buried alive became even more realistic after a few moments in the cramped space. My chest and stomach actually touched the sagging springs of the captain's bed. I couldn't see my watch, so I had no idea how long it was before the police came aboard. It seemed like hours, but it was only minutes.

I could hear them speaking in the strange Ukrainian-Caucasian dialect. Their voices were muffled, so it didn't matter. I heard bumping about and knew that the police were searching the cabin and the whole boat. This went on for several minutes, then I heard laughter. The captain with his coarse humor must have convinced them and won them over.

After what seemed an eon of silence, the captain rapped one end of the board and then smacked the other end. The board fell away and I eased out. The captain had a gruff look on his face. He stood in the center of the cabin, glaring at me, his arms akimbo.

"They saying you are killing a young policeman," he barked. "A man only twenty-four. Wife, two children."

I felt my heart shrink, as though some great hand were squeezing it.

I described the scene on the fourth floor of that building, when I was trying to escape through the trapdoor.

"I could have killed the other one, if I'd wanted," I added. "And later, on the fire escape, I could have killed two others and made my escape before anyone found out. I did everything possible to avoid killing any of the policemen."

He glared for a few more seconds, then a grand smile crossed his coarse, sea-bitten face. "Am believing you," he said. "Now comes more problems. Crew coming at dawn. We go to fishing grounds. You want to spend whole day in there?"

He pointed to the board under his bunk and I thought of a whole day in that dark hole, pitching and yawing on the sea. Even the thought of it was making me seasick.

"No. I'll leave as soon as I'm certain the police aren't looking for me in this area."

He pursed his lips, thinking. He regarded me with a peculiar gaze.

"Police tell of strange thing," he said. "Saying commissar killed up north, near Kharkov, only six hours back ago. Man leave note saying killing being done by Nick Carter. How you getting from Kharkov so fast?"

I was visibly shaken by the news. The American posing as me had done it again, miles away. I calculated the time. Six hours ago, I was just leaving Ilena's barn loft. Only on a fast train could I have made it from Kharkov in time to kill the assistant commissar here in Rostov.

I smiled at Captain Merkolov. "Once in a long while," I said, "Soviet trains make a mistake and go fast."

He reared back and roared with laughter. Then, laughter over, he gave me that peculiar look again. "Police saying no note left after killing of assistant commissar here in Rostov. Why not?"

I told him of the coming of the bus just after I'd shot the young political officer, of how I'd had to go into hiding and then was flushed out by the police.

"There just wasn't time for a note."

He nodded, believing. "Wait. I give more help."

He went to his desk and scribbled something on a piece of paper. At the top of the paper, imprinted in block letters, were his name and the name of his boat. In Russian, he'd written below that: "This man is a friend. Take good care of him."

At least, that's what he said he'd written. I had to take his word for it.

"Now," he said, being the captain through and through, "this is what you must do. There is dinghy tied to stern of *Sonya*. Taking dinghy across harbor to place west of city. Friend have farm. Name is Sergei Yaslov. He will hide you."

He gave explicit directions to the farm, said he doubted that the harbor patrol would be looking for anyone at this time of night, but that I must row fast. No time for leisure.

"You pick up friend," he said, "and coming back. We decide how can perhaps to go Turkey. If not—" he shrugged massive shoulders.

"I'll see you in a few days," I said. "And I'll pay you for your trouble."

"No pay."

"Why not? Don't you like money?"

He laughed. "What Vasily doing with American money? No place to change to rubles."

"You could do it in Turkey."

"Hah," he said with a snort. "Those thieves?"

Ten minutes later, I was in the dinghy, rowing as fast as I could into the dark harbor. For the first mile or so, my shoulder did well. Then it began to throb like a cracked skull. I rowed on, ignoring the pain. Or trying to.

Miraculously, I crossed the main harbor without incident. There were no patrol boats anywhere. And no fishing boats. According to the curfew, no civilian boats were allowed away from dock except during the daylight hours.

A wind came up out of the west and the water became choppy. I kept on the heading Captain Merkolov had given me, but doubted that I would make it as far as he said I'd have to go. I could still see the city lights to my right and knew that I had miles to go.

An hour passed, and another.

My shoulder started to go into spasms. Cramps began to rumble down my arm and chest and back like arrows of fire. Blisters appeared and broke on both my hands. I began to develop new blisters beneath the raw, exposed inner layers of skin. Soon, I knew, I'd be down to bloody flesh.

But I kept rowing. No respite. No leisure.

And then dawn came. I looked around, surprised not to see the low skyline of Rostov. Ahead and to my right was a small seacoast village and I guessed it to be Makeevka. The Vaslov farm was north of that village.

I headed the dinghy toward shore, planning to beach it short of Makeevka. When I was a hundred yards offshore, I stopped rowing and scanned the area. I could see woods and farmland, but no houses. It looked safe.

With bloody hands, I took up the oars again and began to push against the outgoing breakers for the shore. It was the toughest hundred yards of the long, grueling voyage from Rostov.

When I'd finally beached the dinghy, pulling it up a small creek and covering it with branches from nearby trees, I stumbled exhaustedly into a woods and fell face down onto a grassy area.

Sleep wouldn't come, although I was ready for it. I tossed and turned on the soft grass, listening figuratively to the many complaints from my abused body. I squeezed my eyes tight, willing sleep to come.

And then I felt something hard and cold on the back of my bare neck. I spun around, my hand going for Wilhelmina, when I saw the two big holes of the business end of a double-barreled shotgun.

TEN

From my prone position on the ground, the man looked to be about ten feet tall, the double-barreled shotgun more than half that long. He was an old man, perhaps seventy, but he looked strong and confident.

As I lay there pinned down by the shotgun and the determined man holding it, I heard rustling in the woods around us. Two young men came at us from either side. They walked up beside the old man and peered down at me. Each of the two younger men carried a rifle.

"Giving name, please?" said the coarse-faced old man.

I hesitated. If these men were law officers of any kind, the name Nick Carter might set them in a frenzy. If they were farmers, they might be sympathetic. Then again, they might be among the protected, like Boris and Marisa Schamkin. They might want to see Nick Carter turned over to the KGB.

"Name, or I shooting both barrels."

"Name is Nick Carter," I said.

There was a lengthy silence that was unnerving. The two younger men—I guessed them to be in their early thirties—shuffled about on the grass, still holding their rifles on me.

"You have proof?" the old man said.

"No. No proof. But I have eliminated nine commissars who have been cheating farmers out of their farms, who have been sending innocent people to prison, who have been extorting money from businessmen, who—"

"When was last kill?"

I told the old man that I had killed a commissar near Kharkov last night, then fled to Rostov by train where I'd run smack into an assistant political officer out for revenge, then into police who nearly nabbed me. I told him exactly what I'd told Captain Merkolov.

And that was what saved my life.

The old man lifted the shotgun and pointed it off toward the woods. The two young men also pointed their rifles elsewhere.

"Getting up now," the old man said. "Coming with us."

"Who are you?" I asked. I got up, brushed grass and weeds from my clothes and listened to my sore muscles gripe again.

"You must be telling me," the old man said. "Last night, you are meeting friend. He is giving name. You are now telling me that name, if you are the real Nick Carter."

He had me again. If I gave the name of Sergei Yaslov, I might be spilling a secret to the KGB, or to someone willing to sell me and my Russian contacts to the KGB. If I didn't, he might shoot. I had to risk it.

"I am to go to the home of Sergei Yaslov," I said.

"And who is saying such?"

"Vasily Merkolov. He is the captain of a fishing boat in Rostov."

"What is name of fishing boat?"

"*The Sonya.*"

All three men grinned.

"I am Sergei Yaslov," the old man with the shotgun said. "These are my sons, Ivor and Katchka. We taking you to farm, because Vasily is saying so. Also is saying you having something to give me."

I suddenly remembered the note. I fished it from a jacket pocket and gave it to the old man. He looked at my raw hands, then read the note. He nodded as he read.

"Okay," he said. "Coming along now."

They had an old farm truck parked beyond the woods. Ivor and Katchka rode in the back; I rode up front with Sergei who drove. On the way to their farm, he explained how they had found me. Shortly after dawn, Captain Merkolov had called him on his ship-to-shore radio to tell him that I'd be arriving and probably would be exhausted. They had been watching the dinghy for quite some time.

"You wondering why old farmer having radio to talk with ships?" he asked. "Sergei once was fishing boat captain, good friend to Vasily. Retiring five year back, but keeping in touch. Having radio against Soviet rules. Same is with having guns. Sergei say fucking Soviet rules."

"Amen to that," I muttered, as I began to nod off to sleep. I didn't even wake up when the old truck reached the Yaslov farm, twelve miles north of Makeevka. I awoke many hours later on a soft feather mattress in the attic of the Yaslov farmhouse.

Both my hands were bandaged in strips of torn sheeting. I was in a nightshirt and could tell by my own lack of odor that I'd been bathed from head to toe. Even my shoulder had a new bandage. Most of my pain was subdued, but I was starving. The hunger pangs were being stirred by the cooking aromas oozing up through the farmhouse.

It took a few minutes, but I finally got all my parts working right and went downstairs. I met Irme, a fat, jolly old woman, whose relationship to Sergei was never made clear. She was responsible for the lovely aromas of cooking food in the house.

"Just having suppers," Sergei said. "You got hungries?"

"I got plenty hungries," I said. I sat where Irme indicated, nodded my thanks and dived into the most delicious meal I'd ever eaten.

Irme, who couldn't speak a word of English, had killed and cooked a plump goose. She'd also made dressing and gravy. There were several cooked vegetables and even the turnips, swimming in garlic-flavored butter, were delicious. Everyone ate ravenously, as though taking their cue from me. We washed down the food with generous swallows of apricot brandy that Sergei and his sons made each year.

By the time I was finished eating, I was not only full, I was half smashed from the brandy. I felt good. Pains and aches had subsided into limbo. Worries that I'd be caught and shot by a Russian firing squad seemed far away. All trouble seemed remote.

And then Sergei Yaslov asked me the one question I couldn't answer.

"Commissar in this region is bad man," he said, approaching the subject with typical Russian obliqueness. "Has tried many time taking farm. Has come when sons and myself in field, making threats to Irme. Is son of bitch. Understand?"

I nodded. "You'd like me to kill him?"

He shook his head. "No. Saving for myself some dark night. What Sergei wanting know is why you do what you do. Why you come from America, land of free peoples, to kill commissars who are beasting sons of bitches to Russians who are not free peoples? Why you taking such chance?"

Ever since that night in the Soviet Embassy on Sixteenth Street, I'd asked myself that same question time and again.

I hadn't come up with any answers that made sense.

And now I was being called on by my gracious host and protector to give an answer. Sergei, Ivor, Katchka and Irme were all staring at me, waiting for my response. Even though Irme couldn't speak or understand English, she seemed to understand old Sergei's quaint brand of it. I swallowed hard and stared back at them.

"Well," Sergei finally said, "why not coming answer? Is perhaps big American secret?"

"No," I said. "No secret."

"Then why is not telling?"

I suddenly had an inspiration. Sergei himself had given it to me. This man wouldn't turn in the phony Nick Carter for what he was doing, but a sense of pride told him that it was a job for the Russian people themselves, not an outsider. Not a man from a free country who was putting his life on the line for people he didn't know. I had the distinct feeling that Sergei Yaslov would like to see Nick Carter go home.

"I'm going to take a really big chance with you Sergei," I said, leaning back in my chair and patting my full stomach. "Maybe the brandy has loosened my tongue and I'm doing something foolish to tell you, but I think it's time someone was told the truth."

"Truth is good," he said.

The four of them sat fascinated around the table as I spun out the story of how I'd become involved in this wild and dangerous caper. I didn't tell them about AXE, only that an American pretending to be Nick Carter from an American espionage group was stirring up trouble that could conceivably lead to a war.

"I work for the American government," I said. "I was sent here to stop the killer and prevent a war, or even the chance of a war. If I can, I will take him out with me. If I can't, I will have to kill him."

There, it was all out. I'd taken a calculated risk that Sergei's pride would make him accept my story in the spirit in which it was told, make him want to help me, not hinder me.

"You are from CIA?" Sergei asked, his black, bushy eyebrows rising on his sea-beaten face.

"No, but I can't tell you who I work for."

He nodded his huge head. "Okay. How planning to catch this killer?"

"Except for a couple of kills," I said, "all of the commissars this man has executed have lived in the area south of Kharkov. I have a list of them and the locations. I don't know the name and location of the man who was killed last night, but I hope to get it soon. Once I find a pattern in the killer's activities, I plan to stake out the home of a really crooked commissar and wait for this American self-styled executioner to show up. When he does, one of us will win, the other will lose."

The old man nodded, then turned to his sons and Irme and spoke rapidly in Russian. When he was finished, they nodded vigorously.

"Am telling sons and old woman all your whole story," he said. "Am also saying we can be of help. But we do it tomorrow. Is late now. First brandy, then sleep."

Shortly after dawn, we were all back in the kitchen. Irme had prepared a hearty breakfast and we ate quickly. Afterward Sergei brought out an excellent map—also an illegal possession. We plotted the kills and they soon began to emerge into a pattern. When the pattern became clearer, Sergei snorted, blew his nose and cursed.

"What's wrong?" I asked.

"Next kill coming clear," he said. "Next kill must having to be Vladimir Kulinin."

"Is he one of the good ones?" I asked, misinterpreting Sergei's obvious anger.

Everyone laughed, even Irme. "Vladimir Kulinin is beastly son of bitch," Sergei roared. "He is commissar for this region. He is man I save for myself some dark night."

A plan began to hatch in my mind. Even though we couldn't be certain that Vladimir Kulinin would be next on the killer's hit list, we had to gamble that it was. To take some of the gamble out of it, or at least of my eventually catching the killer, I gave Sergei a proposal.

"Today," I said, "you and your son visit trusted friends in this entire area. Tell them you have seen Nick Carter and that he will execute Vladimir Kulinin two nights from now."

"What to accomplish?"

"If this Nick Carter gets the word," I said, grinning, "he'll show up to kill Kulinin tonight. And I'll be waiting for him."

Sergei thought the plan a good one. His sons and Irme nodded their approval. To make certain that the commissar wasn't killed by the phony Nick Carter—in fact, was saved for Sergei and a dark night of his choosing—we arranged for the commissar to be called away from his farm for the next few nights.

I had it figured this way: Even if the phony Nick Carter didn't care whether someone else beat him to the task of executing Vladimir Kulinin, he wouldn't be able to resist being there to find out who this other "Nick Carter" was.

There was only one problem. My hands were still raw and sore from the long rowboat junket from Rostov. Irme spent the day putting on and taking off various potions and lotions. By early dusk, I could handle Wilhelmina if I used both hands, and I could throw Pierre if I had to. But in no way could I get a solid enough grip on Hugo to use him effectively.

It would have to do.

At dusk, Sergei and his sons returned from having spread the word about the upcoming kill. Another farmer, Sergei said, had summoned Kulinin to his farm to show him two goats that had been poisoned. The farmer had sacrificed the goats to make the story appear legitimate. Sergei drove me to within a mile of Kulinin's farm.

I approached the barn carefully, coming up on a side where

there were no windows. After circling the barn, I checked doors and gates, then went inside. I stood in the darkness and listened to the sounds of animals breathing and stomping about. They sensed my presence and were restless. In a while, though, they settled down.

After listening for other sounds, human sounds, for more than ten minutes, I found a ladder leading to the loft and went slowly up. Each rung of the ladder squeaked and complained of my weight, but I kept moving. My hands, covered by lotion and a light bandage, took the stress fairly well.

I covered every inch of the loft, rousing the animals below. Then I settled at a large open doorway facing the farmhouse and waited. In a few minutes, the animals were quiet again. I counted on them to be my early warning system. If the phony Nick Carter entered the barn, the animals would snort and stomp.

In the darkness, I flexed my fingers beneath the thin bandages. They were functioning well, without pain. I palmed Wilhelmina, put on the silencer and took some practice aimings. I removed the clip and actually pulled the trigger on the empty chamber a few times. In a short while, I was able to do it with one hand, but I decided that if I got a clear shot of the killer, I'd still use both hands.

I was just ramming the clip back in and sliding back the ejection mechanism to put a 9mm slug in the chamber when I heard the animals begin to stir. Had the snapping of the hammer disturbed them? I watched the farmhouse and listened to the night sounds.

And then another sound.

Something coming across a field of low corn. I could almost see the khaki trousers thrashing against the green, swordlike blades of young corn. I waited.

And then a second sound.

Two people were coming through the cornfield. Their footsteps were out of sync, and the second intruder was walking several paces behind the first.

I sank back in shadows, but kept my eyes on the barnyard below. The animals were really working themselves into a sweat. Two horses whinnied, a cow brayed mournfully. Goats seemed to be running around in circles.

And still the two intruders came, slashing through the corn.

Suddenly, there was silence. I waited, pressed back against the inside wall, my eyes on the farmhouse and barnyard. I took Wilhelmina in both hands and waited for the two to enter the barn, to start climbing the ladder.

A thought came. I had determined long ago to take the killer alive if I possibly could. But if there were two of them, how could I hope to take either of them alive? Or, for that matter, come out of this alive myself?

I was trying to form a plan when I heard a swishing, almost whistling sound. And then I saw something come hurtling through the open doorway. It landed in the hay, twenty feet from me.

Even as my mind was forming the words, "hand grenade," two automatic weapons opened fire. Bullets whammed into the wood near where I was sitting. I leaped to my feet and charged through the straw, heading for some bales of hay I'd seen when I first climbed to the loft.

Just as I dived behind the bales, the grenade went off.

The whole loft came alive with sound and fury and a great flash of light. The bales of hay were literally disintegrated in bursts of flying dust and shredded vegetation. I felt the concussion ripple through my body, but all the shrapnel from the grenade sailed past me and embedded in the wooden wall of the barn loft.

Still, the automatic weapons kept blazing away.

Although I was mildly stunned by the explosion and its resultant concussion, I worked my way to a small door at the rear of the barn.

And that's when I saw them.

A man and a woman, both wearing khakis. I couldn't see their faces, but there was something familiar about the woman. I had seen her before, somewhere.

My thoughts were torn away from the woman when I saw the man throw something else. It was a miniature firebomb, and it turned the barn loft into a roaring inferno.

I went down the ladder so fast that my hands and feet barely touched the rungs. I started for the door nearest the farmhouse, planning to exit shooting, when another idea struck.

I ran around the open area of the barn, opening stable doors and gates. When all the animals were out of their stalls, clamoring around in the open area, I swung out the main doors and let them free.

As the last animal galloped out of the barn, I followed, Wilhelmina blazing.

The would-be killers were already on the run, dashing off through the cornfield. I circled the barn and watched them go. The woman, running well behind the man, dropped her rifle. The blaze from the barn was lighting up the whole area.

When the woman turned to pick up her rifle, I saw her face clearly.

It was Tania Koselke.

ELEVEN

The next morning as I sat at the breakfast table with Sergei and his family, I explained that things had gone badly because the killer and his woman friend must have been hiding out in that cornfield when Sergei dropped me off in the truck. I'd set a trap and literally sprung it on myself.

And now Radio Moscow reported that the government, at Commissar Kulinin's insistence—and because of the rash of killings in recent weeks—was not only beefing up its KGB contingent in the area, but was dispatching a whole battalion of the Red Army to put an end to such wanton destruction, and to eliminate the American spies who were fighting among themselves for the dubious honor of killing Russians and ruining the Soviet agriculture program.

In fact, according to Radio Moscow, the incident at the Kulinin farm was a serious setback in the country's agricultural program that had been going so well.

But the worst, for me, was yet to come.

Supper that evening was a strained, unhappy affair. There were no smiles, very little talk, but a great number of pointed looks between members of Sergei Yaslov's family. By bedtime, I knew where I stood, and I knew that I couldn't stay in the Yaslov house much longer.

Even though Sergei had been in favor of helping me eliminate the man who was killing hated political officers in the area, and was happy that I'd helped save Kulinin for him, Radio Moscow's propaganda was working on him.

I was the intruder, I had succeeded in stirring up the wrath of the Kremlin and had also made Sergei a target of his own friends. They came, not merely to warn him about the government, but to tell him, in effect, that if he was to be one of them, he'd have to eject this spy—me.

Before going to bed, I had a talk with Sergei Yaslov.

"I'll be leaving tomorrow," I said. "I don't want to bring any harm to you and your family, and I certainly don't want to alienate you from your friends."

He nodded, his dark brows knitting with worry and concern—and even apology.

"Is best," he said. "How you be going? In the rowboat?"

I shook my head. "I don't think my body or my hands can take another voyage in that rowboat. I'll find a way to go."

"Going where?"

I shook my head again. "I haven't the foggiest idea of where I'll go," I said. "But there's one good thing to come out of this."

"Something good is coming? What is being that?"

"If I can't find a friend to protect me, the man calling himself Nick Carter must be having the same problem. Without help, he can't function. He'll either be caught by the KGB or the army, or he'll have to get out of the country."

"Yes," Sergei said, pondering the supposition. "You are right. He is finished."

We were both wrong.

The next morning, as we sat at the breakfast table listening to the radio, the announcer suddenly broke in with an excited, angry voice:

"An hour ago, members of the illustrious Ninth Battalion of the Red Army entered the home of Commissar I. V. Nashenko and found him dead from a bullet wound to the head. The Army was alerted by the Lugansk police who had received a note from a man named Nick Carter, an American spy, who has killed a number of political officers in the Ukrainian and Caucasian areas. Commissar Nashenko's home, twelve miles south of Lugansk on the Rostov highway . . ."

I got up in the middle of the broadcast and went to my attic room. I strapped on my weapons, took the bandages from my hands and went back down to the big farm kitchen.

"I'll be going now," I said.

"Nyet," Irme said, then added a long sentence in Russian.

Sergei shook his head, sadly. "Irme saying we can't send you out for a certainly death," he said, averting my gaze. "But we all knowing is best for you to go. Last night, you saying you don't know where to go. I am calling Vasily Merkolov on radio. He saying you can hide on boat. How you getting there?"

"I'll get there."

Irme seemed about to say more; she was obviously upset, but she remained silent. There was nothing to say. At any time, army units could rumble up to the Yaslov farm, find me and put the whole lot of us in prison forever. I thanked all the Yaslovs for their help and started for the back door. Irme made me wait while she put food into a basket.

The last I saw of the Yaslovs, they were all grouped around the kitchen door, watching me walk off into a wheat field, heading in the general direction of Rostov. Irme was crying.

Five miles from the farm, I saw a group of military vehicles on a highway far ahead. I ducked into a woods, moved south for several miles and then entered open fields again, heading for Rostov.

Although I had no intention of going to Vasily's boat now, I knew that I had to lay low for a few days until the intense heat of the search fizzled out. If Tania and her crazy boyfriend went into hiding, as I was certain they'd have to do, I could use those few days to plan my next action. If Tania and the killer were caught, I'd get to Vasily Merkolov's boat and try to make my escape from Russia.

For that reason, I decided to bypass Vasily and his offer to hide me. He was my best ticket out of this country. If the Russians found me aboard his boat, there would be no ticket. There would be no Vasily.

There was only one safe place for me now. The big question was—could I get there alive?

All day and half the night, I walked across the countryside, staying in woods when I could, and avoiding all homes, towns and roads. I slept in a damp woods north of Rostov, not far from where the last commissar had been killed. Sometime around dawn, I heard sounds and knew that an army patrol was coming through. I skirted out the other side and ran three miles to another woods where I collapsed and slept.

It was noon when I awoke. I thought of waiting for nightfall to travel, but knew I'd need the cover of darkness once I reached Rostov.

The temptation to go directly to Vasily Merkolov's boat and get the hell out of Russia ran high in my mind. It was obvious from the number of soldiers and KGB out looking for the killer, and from the fact that farmers were now too frightened to help the killer and Tania, that the game would soon be over.

Shortly before dark on the second day out, I ran out of the food that Irme had given me. At dark, I saw the lights of Rostov. I had come the long way, circling the city to the north, to avoid having to go through the downtown section along the seacoast. I was still several miles from my destination and there seemed to be more patrols than ever in the fields and woods.

I moved slowly, looking around me and over my shoulder almost constantly. Hunger and thirst became important factors. I'd been parceling out the food in tiny bites, so my stomach was never satisfied. And the only water I'd had was from small ponds and puddles along the way.

Dawn was coming again when I finally spotted the well-kept farmhouse and barn and outbuildings of the Schamkin farm. As tired, hungry and thirsty as I was, I let out a small yelp of pleasure. I broke into a run.

I barely remember sneaking into the back door of the barn and crawling up the squeaking ladder to the soft straw in the loft. I was half asleep by the time my body plunked down in a corner, and I had just enough awareness in me to pull a pile of straw over my body so I wouldn't be seen if Boris or Marisa happened to come in place of Ilena.

Overcome with exhaustion, I slept fitfully. In my nightmare, I'd just emptied a whole clip from Wilhelmina into a huge bat without even fazing it. I had my mouth open to scream when I felt something touch my shoulder, gripping it firmly.

"Nick," a soft voice said, "wake up. You're having a nightmare."

I opened my eyes and there was Ilena above me, her face twisted with concern. The scream that had been ready to explode into the world died on my parched throat. I sighed and relaxed in the straw.

"You nearly scared me to death," Ilena said. "I didn't know you were here. I came up to eat my supper and was gazing out to sea when I heard squeaking sounds in the straw. I guess you were building up to a big scream, so I found you and woke you."

I sat up. My head spun woozily. I could smell the food and the cider and I hoped desperately that she hadn't eaten and drunk all she'd brought.

She hadn't. In fact, she had enough for three people. I consumed it all. Ilena watched me guzzle and gobble, all the time glancing toward the farmhouse and then out toward the distant Black Sea. She seemed to be troubled.

"What's wrong, Ilena?"

She looked away for a moment. When she turned back to me, her pretty green eyes were full of tears. "I don't know if I should be your friend," she said, a catch in her throat. "Even if you have promised to take me to America."

I felt my throat go dry, felt the food begin to churn in my stomach. The look I was seeing in Ilena's eyes was the same look I had seen in Sergei's, and in his family's. It's a look common to people all over the world who are made to feel that they're betraying their country.

"Tell me what's bothering you," I said.

"They're saying such bad things about you on the radio," she said, still avoiding my eyes. "They say you've done such bad things. I thought I understood, but I cannot be your friend if you go around burning up animals in barns. I—"

She stopped. I knew I had to tell her the truth, the way I'd told Sergei the truth. Hopefully, it would be different with Ilena. She was unhappy with life in Russia and wanted to leave. Sergei was unhappy but he would stay and fight in his own way.

Of course, I couldn't tell her *all* the truth. I told her that my name was Raymond Parson and that I worked for an American government agency. I told her about our government's embarrassment at the man calling himself Nick Carter. Right or wrong, Robin Hood or not, I had been sent to capture or kill the man who was killing the commissars.

"With the help of a farmer near Makeevka," I said, "I set a trap for this killer. But he saw me enter the barn where I would wait for him. He burned up the barn and ran away. I let the animals loose. Not a single animal burned in the fire. I'm sorry to tell you this, Ilena, but your government is lying about that."

She looked at me for a long time, then a small, rueful smile played at the corners of her mouth.

"When I was in history class at the Bolshoi Academy in Moscow last year," she said, starting off as though she had a long story to tell, "I was always getting into trouble with the instructor because of my questions."

"What questions?"

"Once, he told us that the Americans were all so poor and that the country was in such a state of collapse that the end was near for America and capitalism. In the very next breath, he said that America was on the brink of taking over Russia and killing us a". When I asked him how a country that was on the edge of collapse could do such a thing, he reported me to the school commissar. I had to go to lectures every night for a month."

"You think the instructor was lying?"

"He had to be. A simpleton could have seen that he could not have been right about both matters. But it happened again, just after I had gone to the lectures. The instructor said that Americans were persecuting communists in America. He said the communist party there was very small and that even the American press said bad things about the party. I asked him why the Americans would even permit a communist party in their country. We certainly would not tolerate a capitalist party in Russia. And, if we did, would we not persecute it in the same way the Americans persecute the communists in America? He became really angry with me. I had to attend lectures for *two* months."

Ilena laughed, remembering. "It was then," she said, "that my desire to go to America grew so fast. The members of the Bolshoi must practice in very cold halls because there is not enough fuel to warm them, yet the instructors tell us that Russia controls all the oil and Americans have none. What is that but a lie? Yes, Raymond Parson, if that is your name, I can believe that the government lied about those animals being burned up. And I will remain your friend. I will help you. But you must not forget one thing. Whether your name is Nick Carter or Raymond Parson, I still love you and I want to marry you when we get to America."

I let out a tremendous sigh of relief. Ilena was still my friend. As for the marriage business, I'd handle that when the time came. For now, I needed this sanctuary to make my plans.

"Thank you, Ilena. I won't forget any of my promises to you."

She leaned toward me, her lips parted, her eyes closed. She obviously wanted a romantic kiss that might lead to deeper matters. I gave her a quick peck on the cheek, although I wanted to give her much more. She snapped back, anger flashing in her eyes. Then, she laughed.

"All right," she said. "Perhaps I am too young to play the role of the vamp. I will let you treat me as a child now, but not when we are married. Fair enough?"

"Fair enough."

When Ilena was gone, I got out the list Sergei and I had made. I compared the kills made by the phony Nick Carter with locations and I reached the same conclusion. After the aborted attempt on Vladimir Kulinin, whose farm was now surrounded by KGB and army units, and the murder of Nashenko, who'd been killed the last night I stayed at the Yaslov farm, the next natural kill had to be either Georg Butorin or Ivan Dushkin. Both men had dachas on the Black Sea, fifteen miles south of Rostov—not five miles from the Schamkin farm. There simply weren't many commissars left between Rostov and Kharkov who were worthy of the phony Nick Carter's attentions. The guy was making a clean sweep—with fifteen dead, counting the assistant I'd taken care of that crazy night on the street in Rostov.

It made sense in another way, as well. The territory north of Rostov was so full of KGB agents and Red Army patrols that the killer would have to go into deep hiding or move to a new territory. Only two commissars had been killed in the region south of Rostov. From what Ilena had told me, they were all just as bad as the ones in the Kharkov area, and even more of them deserved to be eliminated.

I decided that the killer wouldn't go into hiding. He'd made kills at the most dangerous times, including the night after the burning of Kulinin's barn.

So, I would stake out Georg Butorin's dacha tomorrow night. For now, I needed all the rest I could get.

I crawled back into my straw nest and soon was asleep.

TWELVE

The dacha of Georg Butorin was well-lighted. Lamps were burning in every room, as though the commissar was well aware that his life was in danger.

I stood at the edge of a woods, a half mile from the road that ran alongside a whole neighborhood of dachas for important Russians. I'd walked all the way from the Schamkin farm, arriving in the woods just after dark.

This time, I'd kept close watch of any movement within sight of me. I'd passed farms and crossed roads, but with immense care. I was determined to get to the Butorin dacha before the killer and Tania, if indeed they planned to knock off this particular commissar tonight.

Ilena had begged me not to go, fearing that I might be killed. I shared her fears, but there was no choice for me. I went.

But now, I was still a half mile from the dacha and had run out of cover. An open field lay between me and the road.

As darkness fell and became a black blanket over the land, I climbed the tallest tree I could find, settled onto a limb and studied the dacha and the area around it.

Three houses to the right of Butorin's dacha, a man smoking a cigarette sat at a dark window. The whole house was dark, in fact, except for that small red glow. I watched that house for five minutes and saw another glow at another window.

The killer and Tania? Or two KGB men?

A study of other dachas revealed more red glows. That settled it. KGB or Red Army, or both. They'd beaten us all there and were watching the road and the Butorin dacha so closely that not even a flea could have hopped down the road without being in the sights of a pistol or automatic rifle.

I knew the army units would have the wicked Kalashnikov AK-47 rifles. I'd been up against them before. Once, I remembered, a Russian sharpshooter had sent me skittering all over Rock Creek Park in Washington with his AK-47 and its belching copper-sheathed bullets.

Movement to the north caught my eye. Something with small headlights was moving down the field, alongside the road. I squinted and made out the silhouette of a farm tractor behind those headlights.

It was late May. The plowing and planting season was over, and the weeds hadn't even begun to threaten the crops. The farmer couldn't be cultivating against weeds, or even spraying for insects. Not this early in the season.

And yet a farmer was chugging down that broad field on his tractor.

I watched the dacha and those on either side of it. No action there. I swept my eyes back to the tractor and saw by silhouette that the farmer wasn't alone. Someone was standing on the power takeoff hitch behind the metal seat.

Good God, I thought, it's them!

Tania and the phony Nick Carter were chugging slowly into a KGB trap.

My eyes went back to the dachas again. Surely, the KGB and army men inside the other houses could see the tractor coming. No, the road was higher than the field. But they'd soon see the glow of the headlights and reason, as I had, that no farmer should be out at this time of night in this season.

Even as I was thinking this, the headlights went off. I lost the tractor for a few seconds, but I could hear it chugging along in the darkness.

I had a pretty fair idea of what the killer had planned for this night. He knew the KGB and army units were guarding Butorin. He wouldn't be able to use his automatic or high-powered rifles, or his grenades. He obviously had another weapon, something fairly long-range and plenty volatile.

The tractor reached a point directly between me and the Butorin dacha. The chugging stopped. I squinted through the darkness and saw the figure that had been standing on the rear get off the tractor. The figure reached forward and brought out a bazooka.

The second figure sat in the driver's seat and I could hear a faint chugging sound. The engine was idling. Christ, they were treating the affair like a bank robbery, with a getaway car and driver in place.

Smart plan, I thought.

Once the killer had blown Butorin's dacha apart with his bazooka, he'd dash back to the tractor and the two would take off across the field. The KGB men and soldiers couldn't follow in cars or other conventional wheeled vehicles. And the tractor could travel much faster than a running man.

I had to admire the killer. He was more than resourceful and brave. He was damned clever.

But he'd made one mistake.

To escape a killing fire from the road when the men guarding Butorin came rushing out of those other dachas, he'd have to take off across the field, perpendicular to the road.

He would have to come in my direction. The tractor would be abandoned at the edge of the woods and the two would take off on foot. They'd be long gone before the KGB men and soldiers could organize a worthwhile pursuit. In fact, I mused, they probably have a car stashed somewhere on the other side of this woods, on a remote road.

But luck so far was running my way. I was the unexpected hitch in the killer's brilliant plan.

And so I sat on my ass high in that tree and watched the show.

Sure enough, the killer walked across the field toward the road, carrying the bazooka. The driver, whom I guessed to be Tania, sat on the tractor with the engine idling.

While I waited for the holocaust to begin, I checked my weapons. I asked myself if I could actually kill Tania if it should come to that. The answer was "yes." I'd come too far to back down just because she was a woman I'd made love to. But I would try like hell to avoid it.

The man reached the road embankment, paused for a few seconds and then began to crawl up to the road. I could barely make him out. When he flattened himself against the embankment, obviously aiming his bazooka at the Butorin dacha, I lost him altogether.

But he wasn't lost long.

I saw the backflash of the weapon as the first shell was sent screaming toward the dacha. I saw the fireball erupt in the middle of the house long before I heard the sound of the explosion.

Another flash, another fireball, another boom.

I was so fascinated with the man's accuracy and cool action that I almost missed the sideshow.

Lights began to go on in the dark houses. Doors began to open. Men began to pour out. Engines of hidden cars began to burst into life.

And then the man was running away from the road, heading for the tractor. He was running full out, having left his bazooka behind. He ran with amazing speed and had leaped to the back of the tractor before his first pursuer ran onto the road.

The tractor engine roared and I saw the machine lurch and start its turn. They were heading for the woods, for me. But the tractor hadn't gone a hundred feet when I saw new tongues of flame from the road. Men were kneeling, taking aim, firing. I saw the tractor wobble and weave, then get back on a straight course. The firing from the road ceased as the men there began to climb into cars. An army personnel carrier came rumbling up from the road to the dachas.

And then it apparently dawned on the KGB agents and soldiers: they couldn't get off the road and into the field. The men began to haul out of the cars and the personnel carrier to take firing positions again.

Too late.

The tractor wasn't out of range, but they couldn't see it against the dark woods. They began to fire wildly in the general direction of the engine's sound. Bullets whizzed past my position in the tree and I decided it was time to change positions.

I crawled down and waited for the tractor to come to me.

I had Wilhelmina in my hand, ready to do what was necessary to take these two people into custody. I had no idea what I'd do with them if I succeeded, but now I was in the role of having to save them from their own actions.

The attack on the dacha had been a splendid one. I couldn't sell the killer short. He might very well know that I was there waiting, might have a plan to take care of me as well.

But the tractor had no sooner stopped then I knew that something was wrong. Tania had come to a halt fifty feet to my right and, as I ran through the woods to intercept them, dodging bullets that still came from the road, I saw Tania struggling with the man who'd fired the bazooka.

The man suddenly fell to the ground and I knew what was wrong. He'd been shot.

To make matters worse, some brave Russians were now leaving the road and running across the field toward the woods—and us.

I stepped from the woods, Wilhelmina in my hand.

"Need a hand, lady?"

Tania spun around as though she'd been shot in one shoulder. We stood not ten feet apart, staring at each other through the faint light that leaked from headlights of the military vehicles on the road.

"My God!" Tania gasped. "Parson."

"Listen, there's no time for talk. What's your getaway plan?"

"We—we have a car on a road behind the woods," she said, gasping out the words. "But Mark's been hit. He's unconscious."

"Give me your rifle," I told her.

She unslung a wicked-looking AK-47. I took it and went immediately into a firing crouch. I saw the dark figures coming and I cut loose with a blast.

Hot bullets leapt from the muzzle of the automatic rifle. Above the chattering booms of the gun came the screams of men. I had hit some of them, but not all. I fired another burst and, when the clip was empty, I dropped the rifle on the ground.

"Come on," I said to Tania, "let's get your boyfriend on his feet. I've only bought us a few seconds."

She was good at her work. She put aside the shock of knowing that her man was shot and probably dying, and her shock at seeing me turn up literally out of nowhere. She took one arm of the wounded man and I took the other.

We set off through the woods just as another burst of gunfire came from the survivors back there in the field.

I'd made a quick check of Mark's wound and saw that it was high in the shoulder. His shoulderblade and probably his collarbone had been broken, but no vital organs were damaged.

"Don't worry about your boyfriend," I said as we rushed through the woods. "He's only wounded."

"Thank God," she said, grunting under the dead weight of the unconscious man. "And stop calling him my boyfriend. He's my brother."

Beyond the woods, we came to a small knoll. It was hell getting up it, but nice going down. Not only were we out of the line of fire from our Russian pursuers—I could see their dark car parked alongside a narrow farm road a hundred yards ahead—but Mark suddenly didn't seem quite so heavy.

When we reached the car and had slid the unconscious man into the back, I leaped into the passenger's seat and rolled down the window. Tania started the engine and, as the car roared away, throwing up gravel and dirt, I saw six men coming over the knoll.

All six of them went into a firing crouch and I knew that the law of averages was against us. At least one bullet would hit us, the engine or a tire.

My Luger was in my hand so fast that I could hardly believe I'd made such a quick move. I opened fire, raking the line of men at the top of the knoll. Luck or skill rode with us.

All six went down.

"Now where?" I asked, rolling up the window to keep down the roar of the wind.

"I haven't the faintest idea," Tania said. "Mark said he had one last place to use as sanctuary, but he wouldn't tell me where. He said if I got taken alive, he didn't want the KGB wringing the information out of me."

"Great," I said. "Then it looks as if you'll have to go with me."

"With you? Where?"

"Wherever I say," I told her, being deliberately cryptic. "Just take the next road to your left. When we come to the next road, hang another left."

I would be pushing my luck to the hilt taking Tania and Mark with me, but there was just no place else to go.

"He really your brother?" I asked.

"Yes."

"Okay, I believe you. There's a road up ahead. Take a left and hope and pray it isn't a dead end."

"Jesus," she said, shocked, "don't you know where we're going?"

"Yeah, but I'm not a road traveler in these parts. I'm just hoping, like you are."

The road wasn't a dead end. After two miles, Tania took a road to the left and we were moving swiftly northward again. I began to contemplate the logistics as to how I'd pull off what I had in mind. No matter how we planned it, there was great risk, incredible danger.

But then, those things had been riding with me from the moment I'd slid my body into that tool space on the back of that fertilizer truck back in Borcka, Turkey.

Riding with me most of my life, as a matter of fact.

But now I was involving others. Innocent people. Not Mark and Tania, of course. They were far from innocent.

"Shouldn't we abandon the car before we get to your secret hiding place?" Tania asked. "Mark always does that. That's how he's managed to escape capture for so long."

"If we do," I said, "we'll have to carry Mark a hell of a long way. Brother or not, he's too damned heavy for that."

"Then what will we do with the car?"

I shrugged, as though it were no big deal.

"We hide the car with us."

She was silent for a moment, driving along, staring into the distance for potential trouble.

"Know something, Raymond Parson?"

"What?"

"You're crazier than I am. Crazier even than Mark."

"Maybe," I said, grinning and looking behind us to make sure we weren't being followed. "Right now, though, there are a lot of Russian officials who'd have to toss a coin to make a decision on that.''

When we'd gone seven miles north, I figured the Schamkin farm to be off to our left. It would be impossible to make it across the fields in the small sedan Mark Koselke had stolen for this caper, so we had to chance using the road that went past the farm.

"Take a left at the next road," I said.

"Are you sure you know what you're doing? Or do you know, and are you taking us into a trap?"

"Look, since that little shindig where you and Mark tried to wipe me out at the farm of Commissar Kulinin, I'm hardly in the good graces of the Soviets. And, even if I were—''

"That was you in that barn?''

"Who did you think it was, Peter Pan?''

"My God, Ray," she said, honestly shocked, "we saw you from a distance, saw you go into the barn. We thought you were a KGB man or a hired bodyguard. When Mark found that Kulinin wasn't at home, he decided to throw a scare into him by killing his guard and burning down his barn. But you were the one in there, the one who turned the animals loose and drove us away?''

"One and the same.''

After a pause, she said, "I'm glad you let the animals out. I didn't like that part at all, but there was no other way to do it.''

"There were plenty of other ways," I said, trying not to sound too accusatory. "It's just that your brother seems to have his ways and doesn't consider others. I know he's your brother, but I think you ought to give some consideration to just what kind of monster he's . . .''

"Don't tell me about monsters," she snapped. "We've heard enough of the monsters who call themselves political officers to know what monsters really are. So, don't tell me about monsters.''

"Okay. We're coming to the main road. Cut your lights and ease up to the intersection. If the road is clear, take a right, go slow and turn when I tell you to turn. In fact, stop at the intersection and let me drive from there.''

She gave me a look of derision. "Don't think a woman can handle the tough part?''

"You could handle it. It would just take longer, and we have to make this move quick, fast and slick."

Once behind the wheel, I felt more confident that I was doing the right thing. Right or not, it was the *only* thing. The main road was clear both ways, so I eased out, took a right and squinted in the darkness to make certain we stayed on the road. When the neat house and buildings of the Schamkin farm loomed ahead on our right, I slowed until the car was barely creeping.

I eased the car into Boris Schamkin's driveway and moved past the house, the engine barely above an idle, the lights still off. I stopped at the barnyard gate, got out and opened it and drove through. I closed the gate, circled the barn with the car, got out and opened the rear barn doors and drove the car in.

With a great deal of struggle and effort, we got Mark Koselke's unconscious body up the ladder and nestled into straw. I took off his khaki shirt and checked his wound. The bullet had gone all the way through, but had left shambles in its wake. I'd been right about the shattered shoulderblade, but the collarbone was intact. Yet, he'd lost a lot of blood and would wake up to such pain that we might have to strangle him to keep him from screaming bloody murder.

I used my own shirt for a bandage, effectively stemming the flow of blood. I set the bones of his shoulderblade as well as I could in the dark loft. Like it or not, we'd have to wait for tomorrow for more sophisticated medical treatment. Even that would be amateurish.

"And now," I said, after we'd settled Mark as best we could, "I want the whole story, from beginning to end."

"I'll tell you on one condition," Tania said.

"You're in no position to set conditions, Tania. But hit me with it anyway. If it can be done, I'll do it."

"We have to rescue the one person who got all this started. We have to get her out of the country with us."

"And who is that?"

"A distant cousin. Her name is Nadia Koselkovitch. She's only twelve."

"And where is this Nadia Koselkovitch?"

"On a farm up near Kharkov, where KGB and army units are swarming."

THIRTEEN

We hadn't been in the barn loft more than an hour when we heard the flutter of helicopter rotors. Tania was heading for the door to look up when a blaze of lights struck the barn.

I had Wilhelmina in hand, waiting for the first chopper to land. I was just starting to remove Pierre from his lambskin pouch behind my testicles when the lights suddenly went off. The choppers moved away in the darkness, heading south along the main road.

"Just checking the place out," I said, breathing a sigh of relief. "Jesus, these Russians sure know how to make a man's heart do flip flops."

We settled back in the straw. Mark was still unconscious, or had slipped into sleep. The only sounds in the barn were the animals who were still restless, and the faint ticking of the car engine as it cooled.

Tania and I had discussed her strange disappearance from the tavern room in Turkey and all her exploits since that time. Mark, her brother, had come to Borcka to get her and had sneaked her into Russia aboard a stolen fishing boat. They'd dumped the boat just south of the Kerch Strait, where Mark had hidden a car. He'd taken Tania to his hideout, an abandoned farm between Rostov and Lugansk.

And Tania had begun to help him with the killing.

"All right, you've told me what you've done and what Mark has done, but you still haven't said why. How did he get into this kind of business, killing Russian commissars?"

She sighed, leaned against me in the straw and gazed

through the dark doorway into the night. "That's a long story," she said. "I'll make it as brief as possible.

"When Mark was eighteen, he joined the U. S. Army and, because of his obviously superior intelligence, he was sent to special school and commissioned a lieutenant in Army Intelligence. By the time he was twenty-two, he was a captain, one of the youngest in the entire U.S. military establishment, with top security clearance.

"I was just finishing high school when Mark was promoted to captain. We were a very happy family. Much later, when my father got word through his grandniece of things that were happening to his family members in Russia, we were all shocked. Mark took the news badly; he went a little berserk. That was just over six months ago."

"And the grandniece would be twelve-year-old Nadia Koselkovitch?" I asked.

"Yes. It seems that several commissars in the Kharkov-Rostov area decided to take over certain properties belonging to helpless farmers and businessmen. My father had two brothers who had gained a measure of prosperity with their farms. When the commissars failed to frighten the Koselkovitch brothers, they began a pogrom of sorts."

"You mean, they began to kill them off?"

"Yes. Quite systematically, they arranged for various accidents. They killed my father's two brothers, their wives and most of their children and grandchildren. Apparently, they'd decided they had to kill the whole bloodline, and everyone who had married into it, to make certain word of their deeds didn't reach Moscow. Nadia escaped a bloodbath in her home south of Kharkov and ran to the home of friends. The friends found a man who runs a secret shortwave radio in his basement. He sent out Nadia's grisly story and it eventually reached my family in America. That was when Mark began to lose it."

"But he's only been killing commissars the past few weeks," I said. "From what you say, the Koselkovitch murders and Nadia's escape took place six months ago."

"That's true. Mark tried to go through channels to get help from the American State Department. You see, there were still quite a few Koselkovitch family members still living then. Just one word to Moscow from the State Department would have put a stop to the killings."

"And what was the State Department's answer?"

"There wasn't any answer, really. Various officials kept sending Mark's requests from one level to another. The requests never reached the top. Nothing was done. We finally got word that Nadia was the only Koselkovitch left alive, that all the family property was now in the hands of a number of commissars. Of course, other families were facing the same problems, but those families didn't have someone like Mark to get revenge."

"So, this whole thing has been a vendetta."

"Yes. Two months ago, Mark lost his patience with the State Department. He'd been trained thoroughly in the use of various military weapons and had access to them. He began to steal weapons from the army and to lay his plans. He resigned his commission. He set up access and egress routes through Cyprus, but, as you know, the KGB closed that down. You got caught in the crossfire."

"Tell me about it," I said, remembering that night I'd been rousted from my bed and taken to the Soviet Embassy. "And tell me something else. Where did Mark come up with this crazy business about a Nick Carter, a so-called American espionage agent? And why did he leave notes at KGB offices that Nick Carter was doing the killing?"

"I'm not certain," she said, "but I do know that Mark had access to a great number of American intelligence secrets. I think he came across that name in a top secret dispatch and decided to use it. As for the notes, he did that to embarrass the American State Department. After all, they're the ones who did nothing when something still could have been done. Mark has a keen sense of right and wrong, of crime and punishment. It was his way of punishing the American government for the crime of failing to act, to save the remaining members of my father's family."

"Why did you finally get in on the act?" I asked.

"I was in it from the beginning," she said, "but only incidentally. I helped him get weapons shipped to places in Cyprus, helped him set up his pipeline in and out of the country. When the Cyprus thing blew, I was just working up a new pipeline through Turkey when you came along. I didn't know for certain that you were a government agent out to stop Mark, but I had a pretty good hunch.''

"I didn't believe your story either," I said, grinning in the dark barn loft. "The question now is, do you and Mark want to continue this crazy vendetta? Or have you done enough killing to satisfy your brother's bloodlust?''

She sighed and I felt her warm breasts move against my side. She was dropping off to sleep in the middle of the conversation, and yet her closeness, her sweet, delicate aroma in spite of her khakis and the need of a good, soaking-type bath—all these were arousing me. Tania was only a couple of years older than Ilena, but there was a vast difference in the womanness of each. When Ilena aroused me, I felt guilty; with Tania there was a satisfying roar in my loins that told me all was right with the world.

"It really doesn't matter what Mark or I want," Tania said. "He's badly wounded and needs help. And you're the man in charge now. Would you let us go if I asked?''

"Ask and find out.''

She shrugged and her breasts shrugged along with her, pressing, rubbing, massaging my side.

"As far as I'm concerned," she said in a tired, far-sounding voice, "it's finished. Oh, there are two or three that need the kind of death Mark has in mind, commissars who had a part in the killing of our father's relatives. If we get out of here, maybe we'll just make their lives miserable by getting word to them that we're coming back someday. For now, I just want to go home.''

She sounded so sleepy that I lay very still. I had no more questions. I'd let the poor girl rest. Maybe a time for sex would come again. Maybe when we were on the way out, we'd have to hole up someplace and we wouldn't both be so tired. Maybe. . .

She was far from asleep. She was just as aroused as I was. Her hand slid down across my stomach and undid my fly. She felt my hardness, and her hand eased in and brought it out. What followed was one of the most incredibly pleasurable experiences of my life.

●　　　●　　　●

I watched dawn come. I sat near the open hayloft door and saw the rolling Russian countryside come alive with light. I kept glancing at the house, wondering when fat Marisa would come out to milk the cows, when Boris would come to feed the horses and goats and pigs and chickens.

I didn't know just how I'd handle the situation, but I couldn't let them dash off to call the local police or KGB when they saw that strange car sitting in their barn. They'd no doubt been listening to Radio Moscow and would know about last night's raid. Curiously, I began to wonder if Mark's two precise bazooka shots did in Georg Butorin, or if the commissar somehow escaped with his crooked life. And I wondered if members of his family had been in that house when it exploded into fire.

In that moment, as I began to get reflective about my own job as Killmaster for AXE, the back door of the farmhouse opened and Marisa came waddling out with two clean milking pails.

The day had begun.

I left Tania sleeping in the straw a few feet from her brother and went down the ladder to meet Marisa at the door. There was no way to keep from scaring the daylights out of her, but I'd try to soften the blow as much as possible.

Marisa opened the door and walked into the dark barn. I stood behind the door and watched her. Her eyes widened and then squinted and then widened again as she saw the car. She muttered something in Russian and took a few steps toward the car.

I stepped from behind the door and said, in Russian, "Good morning, Mrs. Schamkin."

Marisa's fat body reacted spontaneously—she let out a tremendous yelp and threw both pails into the air.

"Don't be afraid," I tried to comfort her. "I'm a friend of Ilena."

The woman had remarkable composure. I'd been prepared to restrain her if she went yelping and howling across the barnyard. She gazed at me, alternately widening and squinting her eyes.

"Ilena Boritsky?" she said. "Friend?"

I nodded.

I watched the woman's face, saw how it worked. Her mind was also working. She knew that I had something to do with the attack last night on the dacha of Commissar Butorin. She also knew that the good times might well be over if Ilena was ever taken from their grasp. She and Boris would lose the government protection and patronage. The farm wouldn't be nearly as prosperous.

Ilena was their ticket to good times and I was a friend of Ilena.

Even as we stood gazing at each other, each wondering what the other would do next, Boris Schamkin came limping into the barn. His eyes, like his wife's, went through a widening and squinting sequence as he stared from Marisa to me to the car, then back through again.

He regained his composure quickly and rumbled something in Russian. It sounded quite threatening, and I was ready to twitch the muscle in my right forearm to slip Hugo into place.

Marisa began to talk rapidly and soothingly to her husband. She spoke for a long time, and I suspected that she was telling him pretty much what I'd imagined was going through her mind earlier.

Boris nodded at his wife, then turned to me. "Must feeding animals. When done, you coming house. Seeing Ilena."

"All right."

I stood like a rock by the door as the farm couple went about their chores. They were almost finished when Tania appeared at the top of the ladder.

"Ray? Where are you? What's going on?"

Marisa, startled once again, sat on the milkstool and stared up at Tania. Boris came out of a horse's stall and gaped at the lovely woman in the loft. I grinned at them.

"Also friend," I said. "Friend of Ilena."

The farmer and his wife looked at each other and I didn't bother to try to figure out what was going on in their minds. The important thing was to get them to go along with us, to make certain their fear of losing their government aid was greater than their fear of helping obvious renegades. My biggest immediate worry was what Ilena's reaction would be to all this. The girl kept talking about us getting married when we got to America; how would she take to Tania? And I'd said that Tania was a friend also.

"Mark is still unconscious," Tania whispered, coming down the ladder. "I'm afraid he's going to die if we don't get him medical attention."

"No," I said, "he won't die. He doesn't have a mortal wound and he didn't lose all that much blood. But we do have to get him medical attention, if only to ward off infection. Right now, though, all our lives are hanging by a slender thread. We have to take things a step at a time. Boris knows a little about medicine, but I'm not certain if he plans to help or expose us. Just wait and be patient."

I had told Tania about my relationship with Ilena, about the fact that Boris and Marisa never knew that I was hiding in their barn loft. If she had known that the farmer and his wife were in the barn when she awoke, she wouldn't have called to me or shown herself. We had discussed it last night—I was to meet the farm couple first and make all the arrangements with Ilena as interpreter. I could only hope that no harm was done by Tania's sudden appearance, and the thoughts that must be going through the minds of Boris and Marisa.

Tania and I followed the Schamkins into the kitchen of the farmhouse. Ilena was still sleeping, so Marisa went up to awaken her. I don't know what the fat woman told the ballet dancer, but Ilena came down with fire in her green eyes.

"Who is this woman? What is going on?"

I got Ilena quieted and explained that Tania was the sister of the man who was calling himself Nick Carter. And then I had to tell her the whole story about last night. Ilena listened, nodding as I talked. When I had her convinced that everything was perfectly innocent, her quick mind turned to Mark.

"You say the brother is wounded, is still unconscious?"

"Yes. And he needs a doctor, not a veterinarian."

She smiled. "Mr. Schamkin is an *excellent* veterinarian," she said. "He can tell if the wound is mortal and he can set bones."

All this time, Boris and Marisa had been watching us closely, trying to grasp the gist of our conversation. Boris, who spoke a bit of English, was way ahead of his wife.

"Brother has wound?" he asked me. "Where?"

I used my own shoulder to describe the location of the wound. Boris nodded, left the kitchen and returned with a black bag. He started giving orders to Marisa and Ilena. Within seconds, a rag-tag medical team was on its way to the barn.

Ilena explained later that many Russian farmers were good vets, out of self-defense. There were so few actual vets and doctors in Russia that a man or an animal could die waiting for one to come. As for hospitals, forget it. Only the elite of the communist party had a chance of surviving a hospital stay.

But Ilena had given me a distorted view of the Schamkins, painting them as money-grubbing ogres whose only interest was in keeping her satisfied so that the government would continue to send her there, and to send money. They might have had that interest in mind, but they were also humanitarians, with deep feelings for the injured and the troubled.

Boris, who hadn't been in the loft in years because of his age and weight, quickly scrambled up the ladder. We followed, leaving Marisa to stand below, wringing her hands in anguish. I was beginning to like the Schamkins, beginning to be sorry that I'd thrust all these problems on them.

"Must move to house," Boris said after he'd examined Mark Koselke. "Shock. Need warm blankets, soft bed."

With a great deal of effort, we lowered Mark from the loft and carried him into the house and to an upstairs bedroom. I stayed in the room to help Boris set the bones of Mark's shattered shoulderblade, then watched him as he expertly cauterized the wound and bandaged it. He gave Mark a shot of what I could only hope was penicillin.

"Be okay, two, three days," Boris said. "No travel."

Downstairs, Marisa, Ilena and Tania were busy whipping up a monstrous breakfast. We ate in silence, then I told Tania what Boris had said about Mark.

"What can we do, then?" she asked. "The army helicopters were out searching last night. Surely, the police and KGB will start a house-to-house search today. They don't need search warrants in Russia, you know."

"There is a fruit cellar in the basement," Ilena said. "It's almost empty now. I think Mr. Schamkin will let you all hide there until the searchers have come and gone."

"Ask him," I said.

Ilena spoke to Boris. Even as she talked, I knew the answer—and my estimation of the Schamkins went up a few more notches. Boris and Marisa were nodding their heads. While Ilena and Tania cleaned up the kitchen and Marisa cleaned up the fruit cellar, Boris and I carried Mark and his bed downstairs.

The fruit cellar was lower than the basement level and had a strong oak door. Once we were inside, Ilena explained, she, Boris and Marisa would move old furniture in front of the door and make it look as though the fruit cellar hadn't been used in years. It was risky, but it was the best we could manage.

But I had no desire to hide out in that fruit cellar. Besides, there was another job to do if we hoped to be on our way out of Russia in the next few days.

"Give me the name of the people who are keeping Nadia Koselkovitch," I said to Tania. "Write a note telling them who I am and that I've come to get her out of the country. I'll also need directions."

Her expression ranged between shock and gratitude. "But you can't go traveling now. After last night, the whole Red Army will be out there looking for you—for us."

"No arguments," I said, knowing how difficult the job would be and ready to be talked out of it. "Write the note and give me directions. I'll fetch Nadia and be back here by the time Mark is able to travel."

"Travel? Travel to where? All the way to the Turkish border?"

I nodded.

"Impossible."

"I have a plan," I said. "Now write that damned note."

While she did as I asked, I had the despairing feeling that I'd never see her and Mark again. Or Ilena or the Schamkins.

Death lay out there in a Russian field.

And I was going to walk right into it.

FOURTEEN

I drove slowly up the Rostov highway, peering into the distance to spot soldiers at roadblocks before they spotted me. The idea was to get the car as far away as possible from the Schamkin farm.

The day was overcast and that was a help. Pockets of fog from the sea lay in low fields. There would be no sun glinting off the car's chrome to attract the eye of a distant observer. And, at times, the fog covered parts of the highway, giving me a sense of security.

I was reasonably certain of one thing: Mark and Tania Koselke were in good hands, no matter what happened to me.

Before leaving, I'd explained the whole story of the Koselkovitch family to Ilena and she'd translated for Boris and Marisa Schamkin. I watched their faces as Ilena told them of murder by a coalition of commissars; murder of entire bloodlines. When she reached the part about young Nadia's flight to sanctuary with a neighbor, Marisa's eyes were full of tears.

For years, it seemed, the Schamkins had been under a similar threat from the commissars. When Ilena had been sent to them five years ago, the threat ended. But they'd seen neighbors persecuted, killed; had seen their farms and businesses taken over. In the simple telling of the Koselkovitch family story, Boris and Marisa Schamkin had become fans of Mark and Tania.

Ilena hadn't told the Schamkins of her plans to defect if I

could find a way to get her out of the country. She seemed less determined about that, so I didn't know what was really going on in her mind. I'd find out when—and if—I got back to the Schamkin farm with Nadia.

And I'd deliberately refused to tell Tania or the others just how I planned to get us out of Russia. If the KGB found that fruit cellar and took them into custody, none of us would leave if Tania or the others knew of my plans. If they knew of them, the KGB would soon know. And Captain Vasily Merkolov would suffer needlessly.

As for myself, I wasn't all that certain the plan would work. But it was the only plan I had.

My mind was on a number of things, past, present and future, as the car approached the city of Rostov. I'd driven seven miles across open country and hadn't seen a sign of trouble. No roadblocks, no helicopters, no roaming patrols. It was all very quiet.

Too quiet.

I passed a small market, then came to a row of small residences. The street ahead was clear and unpopulated. That was what made it all seem so eerie. There were no people on the streets or roads.

Finally, it became clear. Since the raid on Commissar Butorin's dacha, the whole area had been put under a twenty-four-hour curfew. In that way, the authorities could search homes and make certain every legitimate member of the family was there. And if they did spot anyone on the streets, it would most likely be one of the team of killers that had done in Commissar Butorin.

Christ, I thought, I'm making it easy for them. I had the feeling that I'd already been spotted, that binoculars were trained on me and the slowly moving car.

Ahead was a big machineshop and warehouse. There were no vehicles in the large parking lot and I knew why. Nobody had come to work today. I drove past the warehouse, entered another residential section and turned right on the first street I came to. I went to the end of the street and drove the car right out into the middle of a field.

A hundred yards farther on was a woods. I slipped the lever into first gear and headed for that woods. The car bogged down halfway there. I looked around, my eyes searching for the telltale glint of binoculars trained on me. Without the sun, it was impossible to tell if I was being watched from afar.

Obviously, I couldn't stay there in the middle of the open field. I got out, surveyed the area around me again and walked to the woods. Inside, it was dim and cool. I walked south through the woods and came out behind the warehouse I'd seen on the way into the city.

I had to wait for darkness to continue my journey. I just hoped that no one saw me enter that warehouse where I planned to wait out the day.

Apparently, no one did. I broke a pane in a window at the rear of the warehouse, unlocked the window and raised it. I climbed inside and inspected the whole building. On the first floor, there was machinery, a tool room, a conveyor belt and offices and supplies. A large storage area held crated objects ready for shipping. I opened one crate—carburetors for tractors.

The second floor of the building was mostly empty, though raw materials once had been stored there. In the front section, behind a crude wooden wall, was a long, narrow room full of sagging cots. I guessed that the workers sometimes stayed overnight during the long, cold winters. I pulled a cot over to a dirty window where I could watch the street, and sat waiting for darkness.

I dined on food Marisa Schamkin had fixed for me. I thought of Tania and Ilena, of how different they were. I thought of poor Mark still unconscious from the brutal insult to his shoulder and his nervous system. I thought of the Schamkins and all the trouble this could cause them. Even if the searchers didn't find Mark and Tania in the fruit cellar, what would life for the Schamkins be after Ilena left with us?

My mind was dwelling on such things when the first rumbling sound reached my ears. I peered through the dirty window and saw them coming, a whole line of personnel carriers full of soldiers. They came slowly out of the city and passed the warehouse.

But the last in line stopped as the others went on. Soldiers with AK-47 rifles leaped to the roadway and stretched their legs. An officer began to shout commands.

It had taken them a long time to organize, but the search was finally on. And three soldiers were heading for the warehouse.

I did a fast think. The soldiers would probably break in the front door and never even notice the broken window pane at the rear. But they'd surely search every inch of this building.

The empty second floor provided no protection at all, so I dashed downstairs. I looked around at the machinery and the crates loaded with carburetors. I had only a minute or so to decide where to hide. I quickly began to take carburetors from the crate I'd opened and to place them in a row on the conveyor belt.

It looked as though the workers had finished their day's work with more carburetors to pack. I wanted it to look that way.

I crawled into the crate and burrowed under the remaining carburetors. I was just settling a bunch of them on my chest when I heard something hit the front door. I breathed slowly, smelling the oily metal, and tried to keep my heart from thumping so loud. The smashing sound came again, and I heard the door bang open and hit a wall.

Footsteps of the three soldiers pounded on the wooden floor. They checked the offices first, turning over desks, chairs and filing cabinets. They were doing a thorough job and I pictured them turning over this crate and spilling me out onto the floor along with carburetors. In spite of the noise it made, I shifted carburetors aside and got my trusty Luger in my hand. I'd take at least one of them with me.

The search went on. They were even smashing the tops off the sealed crates to look inside. And then I felt a presence near me, smelled garlic and vodka from a soldier's breath as he leaned over to peer into my crate.

The soldier grunted and moved on.

And then they were upstairs, tromping up and down the empty storage room. I heard them turning over cots. The soldiers soon came back downstairs, kicked a few things around, cursed, joked, and then went outside. I heard their footfalls crunching away across the gravel parking lot.

Much later, I heard the engine of the personnel carrier burst into life, then mutter away into the distance.

Darkness came and still I lingered in the warehouse, peering out the dirty window. Lights came on in the city. And yet, not a single car, truck, motorcycle or pedestrian went past.

Shortly before midnight, I decided I'd have to risk being seen and caught. I struck out north, heading into the city, in no mood to circle it as I had before. Besides, there was just as much chance of being caught in the open fields as in the city itself. Probably more.

The city had been searched, no doubt. The authorities would be convinced that the killers from America were out in the country, in a woods or empty warehouse, or a farmer's house. I suffered a pang then, thinking of how the search had gone at the Schamkin farm.

The streets were empty, as I'd expected. I walked in shadows, going swiftly. If people were watching, I had the feeling they would be too frightened to say anything. In such a climate of fear, who wanted to draw attention to himself, especially when the danger from the Americans (me, Tania and Mark) was moving swiftly away?

I did avoid the downtown section, keeping to residential and industrial areas. In just two hours, I was on the northern edge of town, moving toward the abandoned farm Mark Koselke had used as his hideout. I'd decided to give myself an extra bit of protection by cadging some of his lightweight weapons.

It was easy to see why the farm had been abandoned. The farmhouse was a shambles, with all its windows broken out. A huge hole in the roof let in the elements, and the ancient chimney had started to collapse sideways into the house itself. I circled the house and found a barn in even worse condition. Behind the barn, though, was a small shed that seemed to have fared better. I opened the door of the shed and went in.

The shed was packed with bazookas, mortars, automatic rifles, high-powered rifles, grenades, and box upon box of ammunition for all the weapons. He even had a compact flame thrower.

Suddenly, something didn't seem right. The shed was small, but it had seemed bigger from the outside. The room where Mark Koselke had his weapons stashed was smaller than the overall shed. But there was no door in the rear wall.

I went outside and circled the shed. Sure enough, there was another outer door. I opened it onto a tiny cubicle and saw a piece of salvation in there.

It was a motorcycle with a sidecar. On a shelf above the bike were two cans of gasoline. Ideas began to click in my head.

I closed the shed door and moved on north.

Shortly before four A. M., I came to the farm of Anatoly and Wanda Cherlovitch, the neighbors who had given a haven to the frightened, fleeing Nadia Koselkovitch. I liked these people without even knowing them.

I went boldly up on the porch and knocked on the door. A few minutes later, a light went on inside. The door opened, and a small man with a beard regarded me. He had tiny, twinkling eyes and wore an old-fashioned nightshirt.

He let out a stream of Russian. I could make out just enough to know that he was complaining about another search. There was nobody here, he said, but himself, his wife and his young daughter.

I tried a little Russian on him, saw the perplexed look in his face and handed him the note Tania had written. He closed the door and I saw him go over to a lamp and read the note. Even through the lace-curtained window, I could see his face go white. I heard him calling for Wanda, then saw a heavyset woman come down in a similar nightshirt.

The door finally opened again. Anatoly Cherlovitch looked up and down the empty road and yanked me inside.

"'Merica?" he asked. "Tak Nadia to 'merica?"

I nodded.

The old woman burst into tears, but she responded with alacrity when her husband told her to get Nadia. "Hurry, hurry," he kept yelling in Russian.

Three minutes later, while I was sipping apricot brandy the old man had poured for us, Wanda came downstairs with an exceptionally pretty little girl. It was Nadia, but she looked much younger than twelve, except for the tiny bubbles behind her shirt, where breasts were beginning to form. She had wide, lovely eyes, like Tania. She was going to be a great beauty like her cousin.

The old woman cried and cried, touching off Nadia who bawled as though her life were about to end. The old man began to sniffle and I had to turn away to keep from joining in.

"Do you speak English, Nadia?" I asked.

"A little," she said in a small, sweet voice. "Learning in school."

"All right. Listen to me. Listen well. If you don't understand everything I'm saying, ask me to repeat. Okay?"

She smiled and I saw Tania all over her face. "Okay," she said.

I told her that we had a few miles to walk, but that then we'd have a motorcycle. If we were stopped by a patrol, she was to do the talking. She was to say that I was her uncle, that I was a deaf mute. She was to say that she had a fierce pain in her side and we thought it was appendicitis. I was taking her to a hospital in Rostov. If the story didn't hold up, I told her, we'd make a run for it and there might be great danger.

She repeated the story in English, then said it in Russian to the Cherlovitches. The old farmer and his wife nodded, agreeing that the story sounded plausible.

After a tearful farewell, Nadia and I trudged off down the road in the pre-dawn darkness. I was busy calculating the time it would take us to run that motorcycle across back roads, avoiding the city, and getting within easy walking distance of the Schamkin farm. In a straight line, it was less than thirty miles. A circuitous route would make it closer to fifty. And with the bad secondary roads, we might bomb out on the motorcycle and never make it.

For a time, as we walked along, Nadia was quiet. She carried her few belongings in a cheap overnight bag which she clutched to her budding bosom. She walked purposefully, with a disciplined determination. It was easy to see why she was the one to have survived the plot of the greedy commissars in this region. I wondered how many had not survived. Tania hadn't said how many in the Koselkovitch family had been killed.

I asked Nadia about that.

She looked up at me, her wide eyes appraising me, her already shapely lips pursed in thought. I had the feeling that she was still wondering whether she could trust me. Perhaps I was an agent of the commissars, an American mercenary who was leading her to her doom.

"My father and two older brothers were killed the first day," she said. "Run over by tractor. Many times. Then came my uncle, falling from barn roof. Next my aunt and my mother, raped and murdered on the road at night, coming from cemetery."

Her story went on and on. I started to feel nauseous. There were six children in her family. In addition to her two older brothers, two older sisters were killed, then a younger brother. Nadia, left alone, ran to her uncle's farm where seven cousins cowered in fear with their grandparents.

"Night riders came each night," she said. "Much shooting."

In this way, the grandparents and three of the cousins were killed. Finally, when Nadia and four cousins remained, the masked men came and set the farmhouse on fire. As the children ran out, the night riders shot them. Nadia waited until the last possible minute, then didn't run from the fire. She crawled through high grass into a field and escaped into the woods. She ran directly to the Cherlovitch farm, knowing that Anatoly and Wanda had no children. She told the story that was eventually to set Mark Koselke on a rampage of killing.

"I'm still puzzled about one thing," I told Nadia as we walked along the dark road. "Why did the commissars pick out certain families to kill? Why didn't they kill Anatoly and Wanda Cherlovitch? Or, for that matter, people like Sergei and Irme Yaslov and their sons?"

"Because they are not Polish," Nadia said. "The commissars know that all Russians hate Poles, and all Poles hate Russians. They killed Poles, like us."

"You're Polish?"

"I am Russian," she said. "My father was Russian. My grandfather was Russian. But my great-grandfather was Polish. He came to Kharkov region many years ago. But Russians never forget. Once Polish, always Polish."

We reached the abandoned farm and the shed. I stashed regular and fire grenades, three high-powered rifles, a bazooka and some ammo into the motorcycle's sidecar. I covered these with an old blanket, then rolled the motorcycle outside. Light was just brushing the eastern sky. It would be full light soon. I thought of sitting out the day in the tumble-down house, but searchers might come by and inspect the shed. If we were going, we had to go now.

I kicked the engine into life. The damned thing popped and cracked and backfired like a berserk skyrocket. I was about ready to shut it off when the engine seemed to settle into a low mutter. It was still loud and, by the time I got it up to traveling speed, it would be making a hell of a racket in the Russian dawn. But it beat walking.

I'd already decided that I'd used up the major portion of my luck getting to the Cherlovitch farm without being de-tected. Going back, I was convinced, I'd run into a patrol. If I did, I wanted to have the advantage of speed. The speedome-ter on the motorcycle, an old American model, was set for a hundred and twenty. I'd settle for half that.

"Don't forget, Nadia," I said as the girl settled into the sidecar on top of the weapons and covered herself with another blanket. "If we're stopped, I can't hear or speak. And you're in great pain from your appendicitis attack."

"Yes," she said. "Understanding perfectly well."

I rammed the cycle and sidecar around the barn and house, then stopped beside the road. Nadia looked at me, puzzled.

"One little job left to do," I said.

I took my Luger from its holster and walked back through the weed-choked yard. If Mark Koselke ever decided to start up his vendetta again, at least he wouldn't be able to use the weapons he'd stashed in the shed.

I fired through the open door, into a crate of bazooka shells. Even before the great blast of fire and air blew the shed to bits, I was halfway back to the motorcycle. I leaped on, opened up the throttle and looked back only once.

The shed was gone, but shells and grenades and cartridges were still thudding and popping. By the time the local police or the nearest army contingent reached this noisy place, I hoped to be far, far away.

When we reached sixty miles per hour, I eased back and listened to the engine rumble and roar. The cool dawn wind felt good on my face. My feet liked the metal supports much better than they'd liked the road and the fields. Everything was humming along well.

Until we came within five miles of Rostov.

At a major intersection, two soldiers sat in a Russian version of a jeep. I could see them from a great distance, just sitting there as though they were sound asleep. But they'd been watching us as long as I'd been watching them.

I didn't even slow. I kept the cycle at a steady sixty and waved to the soldiers as we whizzed through the intersection. Through the rear-view mirror, I saw the headlights on the jeep snap to life, saw the jeep surge into the intersection and start after us. I kept going, as though I hadn't seen.

When the siren wailed, I continued on; after all, I was supposed to be deaf.

Nadia played her role well. She reached up and tugged my sleeve and pointed toward the following jeep. I hoped the soldiers were close enough to take notice. I turned, smiled at the soldiers and began to slow. I stopped on the berm and waited, smiling at the soldiers, waiting to twitch my forearm muscles and to put Hugo into action if necessary.

The soldiers sauntered up and said something in a Russian accent that I didn't recognize. Nadia responded, saying I was deaf and didn't hear the siren. The conversation went on and on. I lost the gist of it, but Nadia remained calm. Once, though, when I glanced down at her, there was the look of real pain on her face. When one of the soldiers said something about our papers, Nadia groaned and let out a little yip of pain. The soldiers nodded. One of them patted my shoulder and muttered something in Russian. I smiled, even though I knew the soldier had called me a filthy name just to test me.

Finally, Nadia motioned to me that it was all right to go. I saluted the soldiers, throwing a little idiocy into my deaf-mute act, and turned the throttle. The jeep sat beside the road for a long time, then I saw that it was turning around, heading back to the intersection.

"Good job, Nadia," I said. "But what would you have done if they'd insisted on seeing our papers?"

"Would have shot them," Nadia said calmly.

Shocked, I glanced down at her. She was holding one of

Mark Koselke's .30 caliber rifles. She had the bolt in place and a cartridge in the chamber.

Yep, I thought, this kid is a survivor. We might make it. Might.

We still had a long way to go.

The next intersection was on top of a rise in the ground. As we approached it, I surveyed the perpendicular road in each direction, saw nothing. But, as I was making a turn to the left, to circle the city, I saw the personnel carrier about two miles to the west.

Soldiers were milling around it, waiting.

Waiting, no doubt, for us.

FIFTEEN

"Nadia, give me the rifle with the telescope," I said.

I'd pulled the motorcycle and sidecar off the road, out of view of the personnel carrier.

"You going to shoot them from here?"

"No, I want to use the scope to see what they're doing down there."

She fished in the bottom of the sidecar, found the rifle and handed it to me. I eased around a stand of trees and focused on the vehicle two miles down the road.

There were only five soldiers alongside the personnel carrier. They had rifles slung over their backs, and they were smoking, as though on break. None of them had binoculars or was even paying attention to what might be going on two miles away.

As I watched, other soldiers came out of the nearby woods, buttoning their flies. They had stopped to relieve themselves, nothing more. The only trouble was, the personnel carrier was pointed our way. It would come past us to catch the main road into Rostov.

I calculated all the possibilities and decided on an action. We couldn't stay here. There was no way I could hide the motorcycle and sidecar. If the driver of the personnel carrier saw it, he'd stop and the soldiers would fan out to find us. I thought of going north a couple of miles and waiting until the personnel carrier was on its way into the city.

Waiting was dangerous. Another carrier with a load of

armed soldiers could already be on its way out to relieve this crew.

I waited only until the soldiers had boarded the vehicle and the big truck was moving in our direction. I gave the driver time to get up a fair speed, then I handed the rifle back to Nadia.

"Hide it under the blanket. We're going to dash by them just as though they aren't there."

She shivered, frightened at the possibility of coming so close to a truckload of armed soldiers. But I figured it would be impossible for the driver to turn that rig around until he got to the intersection. By then, we'd be several miles down the road and the slow personnel carrier was no match for a fast bike.

The main danger was in being spotted too soon, in giving the soldiers time to gather their wits and their weapons and to begin firing at us.

There was just enough darkness left to conceal us against the sloping road. I left the headlamp off and picked up speed. Just about the time I figured the driver of the personnel carrier had us in his headlamps, I flicked mine on, turned the throttle all the way and sped past the surprised soldiers like a gnat on a kill mission.

I could actually sense the driver of the personnel carrier hitting his brakes, sense the soldiers back there unslinging their rifles. But we were gathering speed at an incredible rate. I took stock of the road ahead, then looked at the speedometer. We were doing ninety. I eased back on the throttle and glanced through the rear-view mirror. The personnel carrier was still stopped in the road. The driver hadn't made up his mind what to do yet.

"They are trying to turn around in the road," Nadia said. She'd been turned in the sidecar, watching ever since we'd passed the personnel carrier.

I grinned. There would be no pursuit now. In a matter of seconds, that jerk driver would have the personnel carrier mired in the ditch.

But I didn't relax my vigilance. The driver would have a radio. He'd report seeing us, report our location and the direction we were heading. If we were lucky, we'd come to another north-south road before another patrol could intercept.

We weren't lucky.

It was full light when we topped a small knoll and looked down at the long road ahead. Two miles distant was the north-south road I'd hoped for.

Sitting directly in the intersection was a jeep. Even from that distance, I could see that four men were in or around the jeep.

Worse, they'd spotted us as soon as we'd topped the knoll. I slowed and pulled the bike to the side of the road. I looked at the girl.

"Nadia, when you said you would have shot those soldiers back there if they'd insisted on seeing our papers, did you really mean it? Could you really fire that gun and kill a human being?"

"Yes," she said simply. "I can do both."

Suddenly, the thought of turning this twelve-year-old child into a killer seemed a horrible thing to do. Even if she wanted to kill, I didn't want to make it possible for her to indulge such a wish. God knew she had good reason to kill, but those soldiers up ahead hadn't murdered her family.

I would have to figure a way to keep her out of the killing.

And it came to me as I sat there with the cycle engine idling. All we had to do was wait. The soldiers had seen us. They knew we wouldn't turn back because there was a whole personnel carrier full of soldiers waiting for us to the east.

The question was: Would the soldiers in the jeep wait for the personnel carrier to arrive, or would they take us themselves and get the credit, the medals?

There was only one answer. The soldiers in the jeep would take us.

I nudged the throttle and went down the slope at a low speed. The engine popped and cracked on the morning air. There was no fog now; already the sun was coming up behind us, warming the earth.

When we were a mile from the jeep, I stopped in the center of the road. I had Nadia get out and take cover in the ditch. She objected strenuously, but I was bigger and meaner, so she did as she was told. Slowly, methodically, I took the bazooka from the sidecar, keeping my back turned to the jeep so the soldiers couldn't see what I was doing.

I primed the tube and slid the lethal shell into place. When it clicked, I thumbed off the safety and just stood there, my back turned to the jeep.

I heard the jeep engine start, but still didn't turn around. Nadia popped her head up and I was about to tell her to get back down when an idea struck.

"Watch the jeep, Nadia," I said. "When it's a hundred yards away, tell me. Can you gauge a hundred yards?"

"Is it the same as a hundred meters?"

"Close enough."

I waited, listening to the jeep gather speed. All I needed now was for the personnel carrier to come over the last knoll. I'd get one vehicle, but that would be all. And we'd be dead.

"Three hundred meters," Nadia said.

I nodded.

"Two hundred."

Another nod.

"Now," Nadia cried, her voice high, thin and excited. "Now!"

"Not yet."

"Fifty meters!" Nadia screamed.

"Now!"

I whirled around and saw the surprised look on the jeep driver. He and his front seat passenger saw the bazooka. The driver hit the brakes at the same time I pulled the trigger.

The bazooka tube jerked hotly in my hands and slammed against my sore shoulder. I saw the projectile leap from the muzzle in a great tongue of flame. I was leaning over the sidecar to snatch up another shell when the boom came.

I was already falling back when the concussion reached me. I smacked the pavement just as the roar nearly burst my eardrums. Direct hit. The jeep and its occupants were invisible in the midst of a gigantic fireball. A second explosion ripped through the quiet morning as the gas tank caught.

"Keep your head down," I screamed at Nadia. "Keep down."

I'd yelled just in time. The girl was so fascinated by the fireball and twin explosions that she'd climbed halfway to the road. Just as she slammed her thin body back to the ground, a huge snarl of hot shrapnel zinged past her, close enough to singe her hair.

And then the flaming, smoldering body of a mangled soldier landed on the berm right beside the motorcycle. I saw two burning jeep tires spinning along the ditch and into the open field.

I took one quick look at the jeep, its skeleton now visible through the lashing flames, and saw that we had nothing further to worry about. The other three soldiers were gone, either blown into the ditches or consumed by the intense heat.

"Come on, Nadia. We have to hurry."

When she didn't respond, I went to the side of the road and saw why. She was bending over, losing everything she'd eaten in the past ten or twelve hours.

Ten minutes later, we were breezing south again. Nadia, pale as a ghost, leaned back in the sidecar, her eyes closed. I hoped that she was asleep and that her sleep wasn't filled with nightmares. It was a faint hope. This kid had good cause to have nightmares and, though I couldn't see a way out of it, I was contributing to that particular cause.

The road south was clear, but bumpier than hell. I had to swerve the old bike back and forth to miss the deep potholes, and I didn't make a perfect job of it. Every once in a while, the front wheel would bounce in and out of a hole, nearly jarring my teeth out of my head. Nadia and the weapons in the sidecar would jostle around like eggs in a bouncing basket. Nadia slept through the whole thing.

When I judged that we were within five miles of the Schamkin farm, I found a level place beside the road and drove the cycle into a field. It was dry, so I went all the way to a distant woods, nudged the handlebars between trees and came to a stop well out of sight of the road.

"Ride's over, sweetie," I said, shaking Nadia's thin shoulder. "From here on, we hoof it."

She awoke, blinking at me. "Hoof it?"

I pointed to my feet. "We use these."

She started to giggle when her mind made the connection between feet and hoofs. But, when she crawled out of the sidecar, the giggling stopped. She was so sore from being tumbled about that she almost fell. I held her up until she walked around a bit and loosened up her skinny muscles. The next thing I knew, she had her arms around my neck and was trying to kiss me. I turned and let the kiss fall on my cheek. I held her back and looked into those impish green eyes.

"From now on," I said in very fatherlike terms, "I think you'd better call me Uncle Ray. Do we understand each other?"

She smiled and the smile turned into a phony pout. She was being the cute, coy teenager. "I understand you," she said. "You do not seem to understand me."

I understood, all right. She had a crush on me. I should have known it would happen. But I didn't go on playing the parent. I became the friend. I smiled and kissed Nadia lightly on the forehead.

"Give it a few years," I said, "okay?"

"Okay."

I slung two high-powered rifles over my shoulders and pocketed four hand grenades from the sidecar. Then, we took off through the woods, heading south. Nadia stayed close and, each time I stopped to listen, she bumped into me. Some of those bumps, I was certain, were on purpose. And, I had to admit, a bit flattering and enjoyable. Still, there was no way I was going to let a child her age arouse me.

Hunger and thirst began to catch up by the time we came to the southern end of the woods. We hadn't even found a squalid pond for a drink of water, and neither of us could tell if the small, puffy growths on the forest floor were mushrooms or toadstools.

Beyond the woods were a large field of low corn and a farm. I climbed partway up a tree and saw that a large woods ran along the opposite side of the road.

"You wait here," I said. "I'll check out the road."

She grasped my arm and I thought she was going to try another girlish trick to turn me on. But, when I looked down at her, I saw real fear in those eyes. After all this girl had gone through, all she needed was to be abandoned in a woods while soldiers were out in force.

"All right. Come along. But stay down and stay behind me."

We reached the embankment, and I stood up to look each

way up and down the road. Nothing. Nadia waited in the ditch while I went up and put my ear to the pavement. No sounds. I waited a few more seconds, then signaled for Nadia to follow. When she was beside me, I told her to run.

We both ran. Across the road was another deep ditch and a wooden fence. I crawled over and reached back to lift her over. By the time we reached the southern edge of that woods, neither of us was doing very well. Nadia had a distinct limp, we were both thirsty and hungry and my right shoulder was giving me fits. The rifles seemed to double and triple in weight with each mile we walked.

But luck seemed to ride with us then. Just at the edge of the woods was a small farm pond. The water looked clear and clean. And beyond the pond was a small grain shed. Nadia made a dash for the water, but I held her back. She looked at me curiously—and a bit crossly.

"Drink in small sips," I cautioned. "If you gulp, you'll get stomach cramps and throw it all up again."

She shuddered, remembering, and we went to the pond. We both sipped a few swallows and then I sent Nadia back into the woods while I checked out the grain shed. Again, I saw that fearful look in her eyes, as though I might abandon her.

"Don't worry," I said gently. "I didn't go through all this to find you and then lose you again."

She looked at me with that curious look. "Who are you? Really?"

"I told you, Raymond Parson. And Tania's note told you that I was a family friend who could be trusted. What else do you want to know?"

"You are not an ordinary kind of friend," she said, showing a wisdom beyond her age.

"No, but for now that's enough for you to know. I am a friend and I will help you. Now, wait in the woods. I'll see if there's anything worth eating in that shed."

The shed was empty, but the floor was littered with a variety of grains that the field mice hadn't yet discovered. Chief among them were beans. The beans were small and hard, but they were rich in protein. And we both had strong teeth.

I gathered up the beans, put them in a pocket and rejoined

Nadia in the woods. For the next ten minutes, we alternated chewing on the beans and sipping from the pond. By then, hunger pangs were gone. The water seemed to swell the beans into a full meal.

"I would give a thousand rubles for a piece of Wanda's hot bread with cherry preserves," Nadia said wistfully. It was more than hunger that made her say that—it was also homesickness. I hadn't thought of this girl's future in those terms. She would be homesick, yes, even living with Mark and Tania. Even more, she was in for a cultural shock that would leave her reeling.

But then, I was getting ahead of myself. For all I knew, soldiers had found Mark and Tania Koselke in the fruit cellar of the Schamkin farmhouse. The KGB would have been called in and could have forced Boris and Marisa and Ilena to talk their heads off.

They could be waiting for us with guns and bullets.

And even if they weren't, there was still the problem of getting all of us out of Russia. It wouldn't be easy if I were going just by myself. With three females and a wounded man, the difficulty factor rose to the impossible.

I put such negative thoughts aside and settled down in the woods to wait. I explained to Nadia that we were within a mile of the Schamkin farm, but that we didn't dare go there while it was still daylight. We'd have to wait.

Nadia took the news well. She found a large tree with soft moss at its base, sat on the moss and leaned back against the tree trunk. She was soon fast asleep. Her head kept falling to one side, so I went over and stretched her out on the moss. I covered her with my coat and she snuggled in for a long nap.

I had decided to stay awake, on guard, with one of the high-powered rifles across my knee. Within five minutes, though, I, too, was fast asleep.

We both awoke at about the same time. It was dark. My watch told me that it was almost ten thirty. I yawned, stretched and got up. I walked up and down to get circulation back into my legs. Nadia watched me. I could see her eyes glowing in the light of a half-moon overhead.

"I am hungry again, Mr. Parson," she said, then laughed.

She was a delightful girl, and if she were only six years older. . .

"Let's go," I said, shutting off the thought. "We have a long walk."

"But you said it was only a mile or so." She got up, but found her legs too stiff for walking. She began to stumble around.

"That's if we go in a straight line," I said. "But we have to keep going south, circle the farm and come up from the other direction."

She groaned, but soon got her legs functioning and followed me out into the moon-bright field. We took one last drink from the pond and, as we walked along, we chewed on the last of our beans. As Nadia had wished for some of Wanda Cherlovitch's hot bread and cherry preserves, I began to think of the wonderful breakfast Marisa Schamkin had fixed the day I'd set off to fetch this lovely and precocious— and very courageous—child who was almost a woman.

We reached the farm just after midnight. The place was completely dark. I made Nadia hide in a small copse while I cased the place. There was nothing out of the ordinary. Still, I couldn't be certain. I went into the barn, searched the loft, checked the stables where the animals shifted about nervously, then went to the house itself. I peered in the kitchen window and saw that it was empty. Same with the other downstairs rooms. Were they all upstairs sleeping, or had the soldiers and the KGB come and hauled them away?

I thought of breaking into the kitchen and checking the fruit cellar first. But, deciding that was too melodramatic, I went to the kitchen door and knocked.

Just in case, though, I unslung a rifle and clasped Wilhelmina in my left hand.

After the third time knocking, with twenty-second intervals in between, I was about ready to smash in the door. From above, I heard a window squeak as it was raised cautiously. I heard Boris's quavery voice ask in Russian: "Who is there?"

I stepped back from the steps and looked up. "It's me, Boris. Raymond Parson."

I could hear his explosive sigh of relief all the way from the upstairs window. "Waiting one minute," he said. "Opening door now."

Boris and Marisa were soon in the kitchen, but they left the lights off. Boris grabbed my arm, whisked me inside and closed the door.

"Are watching, am thinking," he said.

"Who is watching?"

"Soldiers. KGB. Police."

"They've been here?" I asked.

They both nodded their heads and, in halting English, told me about the happenings of the past two days. A patrol of soldiers had come just a few hours after I'd left. They had searched the house from top to bottom, but hadn't spotted the door to the fruit cellar. After them came two KGB men and a group of police. They'd searched and asked a million questions. But they, too, hadn't found the fruit cellar where Mark and Tania were hiding. And yet, I could tell by the faces of the farmer and his wife something was terribly wrong.

"What is wrong? Why are you so frightened? How do you know anyone is watching?"

"The wounded man," Boris said. "Is waking while KGB in house. Is making groan."

"Did the KGB men hear him?"

Boris shrugged. "Seeing fear in faces, me and Marisa. Is knowing, so is watching house from afar."

"All right," I said, trying to calm them. "I'll find a way to get the KGB off on another trail, then I'll get Mark and Tania out of here."

Boris was shaking his head.

"What's wrong?" I asked, fearing the answer.

"Mark Koselke not going," he said. "When wound is healing, is staying to kill more commissars."

SIXTEEN

"Shit! I forgot something," I yelped as I stood in the dark kitchen and listened to the tale of woe from Boris and Marisa Schamkin. "Be right back."

I left the rifles on the kitchen table, but kept my Luger in my hand as I backtracked through the barn and literally crawled across the field of low corn to the copse of trees where I'd left Nadia.

She was curled up against a tree, sobbing quietly, as though her heart had been broken.

"Nadia, it's all right," I said, putting my arms around her shoulders, nestling her head against my chest. "Everything is fine. Nothing to cry about."

"I thought," she said through wrenching sobs, "that you had left me to die, or to be found by the soldiers. I thought they'd caught you and killed you. I thought. . ."

"None of that," I said, snuggling her close, rocking her back and forth as though she were a baby needing settling after a bad dream. "It's all okay. We're safe now."

I wished that I could believe half of what I was telling her. It was not okay, we were not safe. Not only was the KGB keeping the Schamkin farm under surveillance, but that fool Mark Koselke was determined to stick to his vendetta. Even if I were the coward I wanted to be, I couldn't strike out on my own, save my own ass first. I was tied to these people just as much as they were tied to me.

"Come on," I said, trying to lift her from the ground. "A nice lady is waiting to fix us something good to eat."

147

Her arms clung to my neck and I could see her eyes searching mine. There was still fear in those eyes. There was something else. The girl's infatuation with the resourceful man who was trying to help her was strong. For once, I didn't know how to deal with it.

Because it was unsafe to go down to the fruit cellar at night, since we'd have to use a flashlight, Nadia and I slept upstairs—she with Marisa, me with Boris. Boris, with his constant turning and loud snoring, kept me awake for several minutes, then fatigue took over. I was sleeping like the dead when Ilena awakened us shortly before dawn.

"It is good to see you again, Raymond Parson," Ilena said in a whisper. "I am sorry to tell you this, but I heard one of the KGB men say they would make another search early today. You and the girl must join Mark and Tania in the fruit cellar."

I got up, dressed quickly, and went into the hallway. Marisa was there, in a massive nightshirt. "Not waking girl," she said. "Is very tired."

"Okay."

I scooped Nadia's whip-thin body from Marisa's bed and carried her down to the kitchen. The first light of dawn was just coming through the windows. Boris, Marisa and Ilena went ahead and moved the furniture away from the door. Boris fussed with the rusty old padlock for what seemed an eternity before getting the key to work.

A wave of dank air came from the fruit cellar. In the gloom, I could see Mark and Tania on separate cots, well covered with blankets. At one end of the small room was an old mattress resting on a wooden frame.

I put Nadia on the mattress and she never moved a muscle. The kid was worn out, still sound asleep. Ilena came into the room and, after closing the door, lit a kerosene lamp.

"Put your shirt over the lamp while I leave," she said. "We must not let light show."

I took off my shirt and felt the coolness of the dank cellar. I marveled that Mark and Tania were still alive. This place was a haven for people who wanted to die of pneumonia. Ilena gazed fondly at me, then went outside. As I was putting on my shirt, I heard the old lock snap in place, heard them moving furniture about. I looked around the room, with its sagging shelves of canned fruits and vegetables and a thought came to mind: sanctuary or tomb?

Well, we'd soon find out.

I acquanted myself with the room, blew out the lamp to conserve both oxygen and fuel and lay on the mattress beside Nadia. I covered us both with my jacket and went immediately back to sleep.

I was awakened by a distant thumping. I heard Mark Koselke moan from his cot not far from me. The thumping grew louder, followed by heavy footfalls through the house.

"What is that?" Nadia asked in her high-pitched voice.

"Shhhh," I said. "I think the KGB has come for another search." And then came another voice, in a whisper:

"Ray, is that you?"

"It's me Tania. I have Nadia with me. Be still and keep Mark quiet. The searchers are back."

We lay there in silence, listening to the many footfalls on the floor above us. Every once in a while, Mark would start to moan. I could hear the moan become muffled and knew that Tania was putting her hand over his face. Beside me, Nadia began to tremble and I took her into my arms to calm her.

I was dying to know what time it was, but it was impossible to see my watch in the blackness of the fruit cellar. The searching seemed to go on forever. Once in a while, I'd hear a voice, loud and threatening. Then would come a soft, calm voice and I knew that it was Ilena standing up to the bullying KGB agents.

At least an hour passed before I heard footfalls on the cement steps to the basement. Mark started to groan, but Tania cut him off almost immediately. I got up from the mattress and went to his side. If necessary, I knew, I'd have to cover his mouth and nose both, cut off his air completely. If I suffocated him, Tania would never forgive me. On the other hand, if the searchers heard his moans and groans, we'd all be dead. And that included Ilena and the Schamkins.

The search of the basement seemed cursory. At least, it didn't last long. When I heard footfalls going back upstairs, I tried to count the number. It would be just like them to leave one man behind, to listen, to hope that anyone hiding down here would feel safe and would come out.

Mark moaned and I pushed Tania's hand away. I clasped my hand over his mouth, my fingers over his nostrils. He started to thrash on the cot and I put my mouth close to his ear and shushed him.

"One sound and they'll kill us all," I whispered. "Now, stop the damned moaning."

"Who. . ."

I cut off his question with my hand and fingers, relaxing them only when I was convinced that Mark would suffocate in a few more seconds. He was still. Apparently, my message had gotten through.

After another hour, during which the house was deathly quiet, I heard footfalls again on the cellar steps. Then, the furniture was being moved about, then a key was diddling once more at the rusty padlock. The door swung open, squeaking in protest, and fresh air washed in on us.

"Are you all right?" Ilena asked.

"For moles, we're fine," I said, grinning out at her. "For human beings, I think we might have cause for complaint."

Ilena lit the kerosene lamp and I was surprised to see Mark Koselke sit up on his cot. Boris and Marisa had said he'd been conscious yesterday and had threatened to go on with his killing when he was well, but I hadn't expected him to progress so far so rapidly. He sat on the cot and smiled at Ilena. Her return smile spoke volumes.

In the two days that Ilena had taken care of Mark Koselke, she'd found another love. Frankly, I breathed a sigh of relief.

"The Schamkins say it's safe for you to come upstairs now," Ilena said, looking at Mark and not at the rest of us. "She's fixing a fine breakfast, although it's almost noon."

While Tania and Ilena helped Mark upstairs, I followed behind with Nadia. In the big kitchen, Nadia was formally introduced to her American cousins. She turned suddenly shy, curtsied, spoke her best textbook English and was as charming as a koala bear.

Mark reached out and put his hand around Nadia's small neck, pulled her close and kissed her full on the lips. In that moment, I lost Nadia as well. The full force of her infatuation was turned to her cousin, the man who'd come to avenge the deaths of her family.

It was the second sigh of relief for me that morning. There was still Tania, but I'd known for some time that her attentiveness had been only because she was trying to use me to get safely through Turkey and to the Russian border.

After breakfast, a happy affair for most everyone but me and Boris Schamkin, I got the farmer aside in the little sitting room in the front of the house. I peered up and down the road, saw no sign of anyone waiting or watching and turned to face the stocky farmer.

"I have a plan to get us out of Russia," I said, "but there are some problems."

"Yes?"

"First, I have to get us into Rostov, to the wharves. I met a fishing captain there and I'm hoping he'll still be willing to help, but I can't be certain."

"Perhaps can be helping," Boris said. "Is another problem?"

"Yes, Ilena wants to defect to America. I promised her that I'd take her with me."

He merely nodded.

"If she goes," I said, "won't the government get nasty with you? After all, you and Marisa are kind of official guardians for her when she's on vacation."

"Would be big trouble," Boris said. "Must doing what is best for Ilena."

I nodded. The man had ten times the courage Ilena had credited him for. If Ilena left with us—whether we made it or not—there would be more than big trouble for Boris and Marisa Schamkin.

"You could lose your farm," I said. "They could send you and Marisa to separate work camps up north."

"Am knowing this," he said, then added something that really endeared him to my heart. "Am feeling guilty because of government help. Friends, neighbors unhappy with us. Getting privileges while they getting nothing. Marisa and myself, both having guilts. Not caring what happen with us, just so Ilena come happy."

"Just so you know the consequences," I said. "I didn't want to sneak Ilena away from here without your knowledge and consent. You've both been good to me—to us. I don't want to trick you."

"An understanding. Am thanking you."

"No, Boris," I said. "It is I who am thanking you."

He smiled, nodded his head and kept on nodding. "We being friends," he said. "First friend in long time."

I shook his hand, proudly. "Now, for a third problem," I said. "Mark Koselke still insists he will stay and continue the killing. I can't let that happen, even if I have to kill him. If we try to make him go, he'll surely put up a fight somewhere along the line and cause us to fail in our escape plan."

Boris grinned. "Is no problem."

I wasn't so sure, but I let it drop. "Now, for another problem. There is no way I can do this alone. I need help to get us all to Rostov, to the fishing boat. I have an idea that might work, but it would mean more help and sacrifice from you—and great danger to you and Marisa."

"Saying it, friend," he said. "Am helping what can do."

I told him the plan, slowly, using simple words, making it as plain as possible. When I was finished, he started the nodding again. He pursed his lips, gripped his hands together, got up and paced the room. He peered through the curtains at the road, then turned to face me.

"Is good plan. Must be doing now. Soldiers not suspecting trick in daytime."

"All right," I said. "We'll set it in motion. Do you want me to do the killing?"

"No. Am doing that myself."

SEVENTEEN

Boris Schamkin and I said nothing to the others about my plan. We went out to the barn where we gathered up tools, then walked across to the open-ended shed and the old farm wagon. Boris took down several boards he had stashed in the rafters.

We measured the bed of the wagon and Boris sawed the boards off at the desired length. By mid-afternoon, we had a whole new floor in the wagon, about eighteen inches above the regular floor.

I'd gotten the idea from that miserable ride in the fertilizer truck from Borcka to Tiflis. We were building a secret compartment to hide people, but the load on top wouldn't be fertilizer.

"Now," Boris said, peering into the long, shallow compartment we'd created, "must be coming final touch."

If he simply nailed a board over the end of the wagon, any fool would know that the wagon had a false bottom, and would pry the board loose and look in. Boris measured the opening and cut a board to fit into it. He tapped it back about two feet from the end of the wagon and, from the inside to conceal the nailheads from outside observation, he nailed the board in place.

This left a space about two feet deep, eighteen inches high and as wide as the wagon at the rear. We lugged cartons of canned fruit and vegetables from the fruit cellar and packed them into the space.

"Will be giving away some to soldiers as bribes," Boris said, grinning. "Still having plenty left at end of trip."

Our story on the canned food was that Boris was taking it to the home of a commissar in Rostov. Even so, we could expect a few soldiers to want a jar or two—which, with a wink, Boris would say the commissar would never miss.

The next job was to knock out the wagon's front board. Through that opening, Mark, Tania, Nadia, Ilena and I would crawl, to hide in the space just ahead of the compartment containing the canned food. Boris put in a thick layer of straw to make our trip easier. Once we would be crammed into the space, Boris would nail the front board back where it belonged.

If all went well, we'd be safe until we reached our destination. We'd planned to leave so that we'd arrive at the Rostov wharves just before dark. Boris and his wife would spend the night with friends—there was still one couple who kept in touch with the "rich" farmer who was a surrogate parent to a Bolshoi Ballet member—and return alone the next day.

"It will work, Boris," I said. "But there's that other problem before we get to the killing."

"What being problem?"

"Mark Koselke," I said. "I'd like to know what you have in mind for him."

Boris grinned. "Remembering needle Boris using for killing infection in Mr. Koselke?"

I nodded.

"Same needle can be using for, how you say, putting to sleep?"

"A knockout drug? Wonderful. Give him enough to last a long time, Boris. I don't want him yelling his head off while we're carrying him aboard the fishing boat."

"Not to worry." His grin was almost evil.

But I *was* worrying, not about Mark because I knew this old veterinarian would put Mark into sleepyland for a long time. Other questions nagged at me.

The plan seemed to be perfect. I'd gotten it after remembering that powerful odor when I was making my way along the wharves in Rostov and had seen the low building and the sign in Russian. I'd been able to make out the word "slaughterhouse." Boris had confirmed that a slaughterhouse existed there, that he'd taken animals to it from time to time.

Still, I was bothered by loose ends we might have forgotten.

"I just thought of something," I said as we admired the job we'd done on the wagon. "If someone asks why you killed your own cow, what will you tell them?"

"Am saying cow broke leg, am having to put her from misery."

"Okay, but if any of the soldiers look closely, they'll see that the cow's leg isn't broken."

Boris shrugged. "Okay, is breaking leg after cow is dead, when not feeling pain."

I grinned, wishing I'd thought of that. Still, I was bothered.

"One more thing, Boris," I said. "Ilena. I think she should ride topside with you and Marisa. If we're stopped by the same guards who searched your house twice, they'll wonder where she is."

"Is good point," he said. "Wishing am thinking of it myself. Got more problems in head?"

I've got a lot of problems in my head, I thought, or I wouldn't be here in the first place. As convinced as I was that it was a good plan, there were just too many places where it could go wrong. And, in spite of this man's obvious courage, I was already grieving over what would happen to him and his wonderful wife after we were gone, after Ilena had defected.

"None that I'd like to discuss," I replied. "Let's tell the others the plan and get moving."

He nodded, and we went into the house. He was no longer limping.

As expected, Mark Koseke disagreed with everything we'd planned. Well, not everything. He wanted me to take Tania and Nadia with me, but he had no intentions of going himself. And when I mentioned that Ilena planned to defect, she got a strange look on her face.

Marisa didn't object to the plan, but her face plainly showed that she hated losing her beloved cow. But she knew that, without the cow lying in the bed of the wagon—and us hiding beneath the newly laid floor—the whole trip would be useless. It was vital that our destination be the wharves of Rostov, and that's where the slaughterhouse was.

As for Mark, Boris assured him time and again that he didn't have to go. He could stay in the house as long as he needed. But, to make certain he didn't get infection in his shoulder, or catch pneumonia hiding down in that damp fruit cellar, Boris would give him another shot of penicillin just before the rest of us left.

"If Mark does not go," Nadia said, her pretty little chin sticking out a mile, "I also am not going."

Mark looked at her, smiling gently. "You must go, little flower. Otherwise, what I've done here—and will continue to do—will have been a waste."

I could have told him his actions had been a waste all along, but there was still that one thread of sympathy remaining.

"I can shoot a gun," Nadia persisted. "Ask Mr. Parson if I was not ready to kill when it was necessary."

"You were ready," I said, "and you would have done it. But Mark is right. You haven't been spared to turn into a killer, even for revenge. I think you'd better do what your cousin says to do."

She was about to resist more, but she looked from me to Mark and back again. It was clear that her maturing emotions were being torn.

"I will go," she mumbled.

I looked at Ilena to see if she had anything to say. She still looked angry at me for telling Boris of her plans to defect, but she also seemed to be regarding her guardians in another light. Here she was planning to do something that would bring great harm to them and they were going to help her do it. I could tell that Ilena's own emotions were churning about, making her indecisive.

"It's time we got going," I said. "It's almost five o'clock and we want to reach the wharves just about dark."

Once again, I offered to do the killing, but Boris merely shook his head.

"You would be shooting with rifle. Soviet citizens not

allowed for having guns. Some having guns, but taking big risk. Boris not having gun.''

"Then, how will you kill the cow?''

"Using time-honored way of fathers and grandfathers,'' he said sadly. "Using sledgehammer between eyes. Is quick and painless.''

I wondered how he knew it was painless. Just the thought of it gave me a tremendous headache. I watched through the window, wondering how he'd get the dead cow onto the wagon. The sharp old guy let the cow do the work. He laid three planks against the back of the wagon and led the cow up. He kicked aside the planks, climbed onto the front of the wagon and, with only a moment's hesitation, smashed the animal squarely between the eyes.

I turned my head then. I couldn't watch the next step in the plan, even though I knew the cow would not feel the pain of its leg being broken.

Back in the kitchen, Boris washed his hands carefully and went for his medical bag. He took out a syringe, filled it with liquid and told Mark to roll up his right sleeve. Mark, thinking he was getting a shot to ward off infection, dutifully rolled up his sleeve and winked at Nadia who was looking a bit pale from the sight of the needle.

"See there, Nadia,'' Mark said, as he rolled down his sleeve. "Needles don't hurt. It's all in your mind. When it's necessary for you to have injections, you must. . .''

I caught him as his eyes rolled back in his head and he tumbled out of the chair.

"My God,'' Tania exploded. "What happened?''

"Something to keep him quiet until we're out to sea,'' I told her.

"But you're taking him against his will,'' she cried.

"Would it be better to leave him here to be hunted down and killed?'' I demanded. "Damn it, Tania, he's done enough killing. We all have. It's over. All the political officers who had anything to do with the genocide of the Koselkovitch family are dead. Mark was spreading out to others just to make sure. He'd caught the bloodlust and couldn't stop. Is that what you want for your brother?''

She looked at me and at her unconscious brother. I'd laid Mark on the kitchen floor where he was sleeping with a blissful look on his face.

"But he'll be put in prison when we get to the States," Tania said.

"Not likely," I said. "As far as America is concerned, his greatest crime—and yours—has been leaving and entering the country with fake passports. As a member of the government, I think maybe I can have that minor problem taken care of. Even if you both have to spend a few months in jail, isn't it better than what's waiting for him out there?" I swept my arm around, to take in the whole of Russia.

"But you tricked him," Tania said petulantly.

"Jesus, kid," I snapped. "If you want to start discussing the department of trickery, let's go back to when you first sat beside me on that Air Turk flight from London. Let's—"

"Point made," she said, almost smiling. "Let's get going."

The ride wasn't nearly as agonizing as I'd expected it to be.

Boris had hitched his two horses to the wagon and, shortly after five P. M., we were on the main road to Rostov. The road was fairly smooth.

In our space, we had plenty of light and air through the cracks between the boards of the old wagon. The straw was thick enough to keep our bones from being jostled against the floor. I was sandwiched between Tania and Nadia, and we'd put Mark crossways in the wagon, up near the fake back. Ilena, as I'd suggested, rode topside between Boris and Marisa.

We hadn't gone two miles, though, before we were stopped by a patrol. I listened to feet crunching on the gravel and guessed there to be four or five soldiers in the group. I couldn't make out a fraction of their language, but we were on our way sooner than I'd expected.

After we were well along, Tania told me what had been said.

"They asked Boris why he was in such a hurry to take the cow to the slaughterhouse if she'd only broken her leg today," Tania told me.

"And what did Boris say?"

She giggled. "He said dead cows sometimes explode a few hours after they die and asked if they'd like cowshit and guts splattered all over them. He said the cow was about to pop any minute. They backed off in a hurry."

Good old Boris, I thought. Too bad he didn't want to defect. Hawk would love the guy.

The slaughterhouse crew seemed overjoyed to get the cow. Boris received his pay and started up the wagon again. It was dark in the space, so we knew it was dark outside. I had given Boris directions to the pier where *The Sonya* was tied up.

The wagon stopped and Boris got off. I waited to hear the footfalls of another patrol, but everything was quiet outside. I could hear the distant toot of a horn and knew it to be a foghorn in the harbor. Christ, I thought, there's a fog. I hoped my old friend, Vasily Merkolov, was an excellent navigator. If he were, the fog would be a godsend, protecting us from view. If not, we were in for trouble trying to get through the harbor and down through the Kerch Strait.

The waiting was driving me crazy. I wanted to call out, to ask Ilena where Boris went, to ask what was happening. And then I heard footfalls approaching the wagon. A one-man patrol?

"Mr. Parson," a hoarse voice whispered through a crack in the wagonbed

"Yes?"

"It is I, Boris. Am going to see fishing boat called *The Sonya*. Fishing boat is being at pier, but is no Captain Merkolov. Is nobody."

I was stunned. I knew Vasily lived on his boat. It hadn't occurred to me that he wouldn't be on it. Where could he be?

"Mr. Parson," Boris said through the crack. "What we doing now?"

"I don't know, Boris," I said, my mind ranging up and down the field searching for an answer. "I just don't know."

"Must be doing something soon," he said, his voice showing panic. "Is coming someone. Maybe is being patrol."

EIGHTEEN

I heard the footsteps now.

One man was coming along the street toward the wagon. I reached across in the straw, closed my hand around the stock of one of the .30 caliber high-powered rifles we'd brought along.

With my eye to a crack between the boards, I watched the man come. To my left, barely seen by peripheral vision, was Boris Schamkin, waiting like a man who is to be executed within seconds. What story could he possibly tell the next patrol? That his horse had refused to go a step farther?

Suddenly, something about the man took away all my fear. I saw something in the shape, the swagger. Actually, it was a stagger.

It was Captain Vasily Merkolov, returning to his boat after a drinking bout with a friend.

"Boris," I said through the crack. "That's him. That's the captain. Stop him and get us out of here."

Boris left the side of the wagon. I could hear Ilena and Marisa climbing down from the seat, hear Boris and Vasily engaged in rapid conversation.

Then came laughter.

Vasily's booming, happy, drunken laughter.

Within minutes, Boris had knocked out the front board of the wagon and we were on the street. Vasily Merkolov seemed to sober up just a bit when he saw how many people he was expected to take aboard his boat. Then, with typical disregard of his own safety, he shrugged and boomed in the quiet night:

"Ha, so what, Nick Carter. Whole world full of Soviet polices, plenty KGB bastards, harbor full of fog, now having boat full with peoples. So what. Sergei say you good man, I believe. Come. We set sail now, only not got sails. Got greasy old engine."

His renewed cheer diminished a little when we hauled Mark Koselke out of the wagon, but it picked up again. In fact, he was ready to toss Mark over his shoulder and carry him down the pier until I stopped him.

"Gently," I said. "We have to handle him gently or we'll break all the bones that Mr. Schamkin so carefully set."

"Hokay," he said, shrugging. "You taking one end, Vasily taking other. Gently."

I turned to say goodbye to Boris and Marisa Schamkin. "We really shouldn't stay here any longer than necessary," I said, "but I do want to thank you for all you've done. Come along, Ilena. And Nadia, you stay close to Tania and Ilena. We. . ."

"Ilena not going," Boris said.

I was already reaching to help Vasily pick up Mark. I stopped, turned to look at Ilena. She smiled, a pale, reluctant smile.

"Someday," she said, "the whole Bolshoi troupe will come to America," she said. "Perhaps then I call on you and you help me defect. Not now. I am young, have plenty of time."

"And you know that your defection now would create big problems for Boris and Marisa, right?"

She blushed. "I have not judged them correctly. I thought they wanted only the material things that come from being my surrogate parents. I thought they would report me if they knew of my dreams to leave Russia and come to America. I was wrong. They are wonderful people and I do not want harm to come to them."

I kissed her lightly on the cheek. "Someday," I said. "Someday, when the Bolshoi comes to the States."

"Yes. Someday."

By the time we reached *The Sonya* and had put Mark into

the captain's bunk, the wagon was gone. Even the slow clopping of the horses was no longer audible in the night air. I was proud of Ilena, as proud as I'd been of Boris and Marisa. And, for once, I wasn't leaving behind me more shambles than were necessary.

And who knew? Perhaps Ilena would find happiness in her own country? Meeting a young man closer to her own age wouldn't hurt. And having people like Boris and Marisa Schamkin as her protectors was no small thing.

Vasily and I went to the wheelhouse, while Tania and Nadia joined Mark in the captain's quarters. I'd left one of the rifles with Tania and kept the other with me on the bridge. Vasily started the engine and we moved slowly out into the thickest fog I'd seen in years.

"Fog good for now," Vasily said with a grunt. "Nobody see us. Trouble is, we don't see nobody else."

"How long before we reach the Kerch Strait?" I asked.

"Unless go bang against rock or ship," he said, grinning in the dim green light from the compass housing, "we come at Straits maybe before dawn. Maybe after. Is long way, boat is slow. Ha, you want go fast, you steal airplane."

I'd thought of that, but I knew that I wouldn't have gotten a thousand feet off the ground before Soviet radar pinpointed me and sent a flock of MiGs to knock us down. Radar?

"I hate to ask this, Vasily," I said, "but won't the harbor patrol have us on radar?"

"Sure. Already knowing we moving. Soon make fix on position, send patrol for check. You worry?"

"Hell yes, I worry."

"Ha, forgetting worry. Radar peoples spotting is one thing. Getting permission to make way is other thing. Finding us in fog, even with radar, is other thing. Is many other things. When am saying soon, maybe meaning two, three, four hours. You catch sleep now. Needing you for wheel while Vasily sleep."

There was a wide seat at the rear of the wheelhouse. I curled up on it, the rifle cradled in my arms, and napped uneasily. Nightmares came. Not old ones this time. New ones.

I saw The Sonya entering the Kerch Strait, saw a Soviet

gunboat blocking our way. I saw Captain Merkolov trying desperately to turn the boat about, saw a flash of flame from the gunboat, saw the whole fishing boat go up in one solitary blast of flame and debris and smoldering flesh.

I awoke with such a start that I almost pulled the trigger on the rifle.

"Ah, you waking just in time," Vasily said. "Good sleep, long time. You taking wheel now while Vasily making sleep."

I looked through the glistening wet windscreen at the swirling fog. I couldn't even see the bow of the boat, much less where we were supposed to be going. I looked at the compass and saw that we were on a heading of one eighty seven, almost due south.

"How long do I keep her on this heading?" I asked as Vasily began curling up on the wide seat where I'd had my nightmares.

"Staying that way until am saying different," he said, already mumbling as though half asleep. "Or until we hit something."

He went immediately to sleep. I looked at my watch, saw that I'd been asleep almost four hours. It was strange that no Soviet patrol boat had come to check us out. I'd meant to ask Vasily about that, but he'd gone to sleep on me so quickly. I yawned, presumed that the fog was too thick and dangerous even for patrol boats, or that the Soviets hadn't picked us up on radar because of the fog. At any moment, we were going to ram straight into some solid object out there in the fog and it would be all over for the lot of us.

No matter what, I simply couldn't believe that the Russians would let us go unmolested. It was a long run from Rostov to Trabzon, on the Turkish side of the Black Sea. I tried to calculate the distance, speed and time. The best I could come up with was that, if we weren't stopped, we would reach Trabzon by noon.

Ten hours away.

One thing in our favor was a lack of wind. The fog swirled on small thermals from the water, but there was no wind to roll the surface of the water. The Sonya was making a good twenty knots.

But I kept feeling the way the captain of the Titanic should have felt. There were no icebergs out there, but there could be something. A sandbar, a jutting peninsula, an abandoned barge. A Soviet gunship.

With each tick of my wristwatch, my nerves got tighter. My shoulder began to throb with tension and gripping the wheel. I relaxed, tensed again and relaxed again. Vasily had steered *The Sonya* through this pea soup for four hours and had gone off to sleep as though he didn't know the meaning of the word tension. But Vasily had been full of vodka. I wished for some vodka, but didn't dare leave the wheel to look for any.

It wouldn't have helped. That fog was so thick, so threatening, so evil-looking that all the vodka in the world couldn't have changed it, or my attitude toward it.

The unknowing was out there. I have always been more afraid of unknown and unseen adversaries than I have of those I can meet face to face, hand to hand, head to head.

And then I realized that all my tension came from fear. Christ, I'd been walking, running and riding up and down a large section of Russia for the past several days and hadn't felt this much fear. But I'd felt most of the time that I had been in some sort of control of my destiny. There were the opportunities to bypass the enemy, or to outwit him.

You cannot bypass or outwit fog. Not this kind of fog.

Most of the time, as I strained to catch a glimpse of the bow that was less than thirty feet ahead, I realized that I couldn't even see the deck directly below the wheelhouse. Ten feet away.

All I could see was the glistening glass of the windscreen and a wall of swirling blackness.

I almost cheered, then, when *The Sonya* broke into an open area where there was no fog. Above, I could see the three-quarter moon shining like a damaged silver dollar. Moonlight glistened off the ocean. Far ahead, I could see the fogbank. For the moment, though, I enjoyed the brightness of the night and of the water. I stared at the bow as though it were a lover I might never see again.

And then we plunged back into the fog and fear returned. My hands gripped the wheel until my knuckles seemed about to snap apart.

The hours went so slowly that I wanted to scream.

Although I couldn't see a damned thing outside the wheelhouse, I suddenly had the feeling that we were no longer in the open sea. I felt as though we were moving down a narrow channel. I could almost hear the echo of the boat's engine bounding back from walls on either side. I heard rustling behind me, heard Vasily belch. I didn't even dare turn around to look at him, for fear that I'd steer *The Sonya* into one of the walls on either side of us.

"Ah, now we are being in the Straits," Vasily said, coming up behind me. "You doing good job. I making you captain now, am retiring myself to dacha in mountains. Having enough of this fucking water."

He grinned, took the wheel and made a slight adjustment to the left so that we were on a heading of one ninety four.

"Maybe you not being such good captain. Giving five more minutes at wheel, you putting *Sonya* on top of cliff."

I smiled and felt the tension drain out of me. I could see the deck below and thought the fog was lifting. It wasn't. What was lifting was night. Dawn was coming. It was almost six o'clock.

"You figure we'll be in Trabzon by noon?" I asked.

Vasily looked at me, admiration on his face. "Ha, guessing you are good captain after all. How you figure so good?"

I shrugged. "That means we have six hours of sailing in the daylight. This fog won't last that long."

"Is being correct. Fog burning off in three hours. Be too late then."

"Too late for what?"

"Soviet patrols not coming last night for fearing of thick fog," he said. "Coming three more hours, *Sonya* being in Turkish fishing waters. *Sonya* not allowed there unless having permission. When *Sonya* cross line, come the Soviets to stop. Maybe also come the Turks to make the Soviets go away. Who is being able to say?"

For one thing, the Soviets would have something to say.

More than two hours after the captain had taken over the helm, I went below to see how things went with Tania, Nadia and Mark. The fog was already starting to burn away with the rising sun. And Mark, who was starting to come out of his drug-induced state, was burning up with fever. He was muttering and swearing, as well as twisting, turning and sweating on the captain's bunk.

"He must have ruptured something in the wound during that wagon ride," I said to Tania. "Don't worry. We'll be in Turkey in a few hours and. . ."

A loud Russian voice, coming through an electronic bullhorn, broke off my sentence. I dashed to the door of the cabin and saw a Soviet gunship coming up alongside. The voice kept yelling at Captain Vasily Merkolov, but I couldn't understand what the sailor was saying.

"He is ordering us to turn around and go back to Rostov," Nadia said, her eyes wide with fear. "They will kill us for trying to escape."

Nadia began to cry. Tania peered through the porthole and watched as the ship came even nearer. I had the door cracked and was watching the big gunship. I could see the Soviet captain watching *The Sonya* with binoculars. I could see armed sailors standing at the gunwales. And a three-inch cannon on the foredeck was aimed at *The Sonya's* bridge.

Suddenly, we felt *The Sonya* pick up speed. That crazy Vasily was ignoring the order, making a break for Turkish waters. But we were at least thirty minutes from the invisible line.

The Soviet gunship picked up incredible speed. It shot past us and continued on for half a mile, and disappeared in the fog. Old Vasily continued to pour on the power and *The Sonya* bobbed in the gunship's wake.

And then I saw what the Soviets were planning. They could have blown us out of the water back there, but they wanted to take all of us alive. The KGB must have caught the Shamkins and Ilena, made them talk. They knew that the infamous "Nick Carter" who'd been killing so many commissars was on board. They also knew of me, the "other" government agent. They wanted us both alive, if they could get us that way.

And they had a plan to do just that. As *The Sonya* moved swiftly through the water, I strained to see the gunship ahead of us. It was suddenly there, its engines stopped, lying directly across our path.

The Sonya roared onward, with full power.

"What is the captain doing?" Tania asked.

"I don't want to second guess him," I muttered, "but I think the big, courageous fool is going to ram the gunship."

The headlong plunge of *The Sonya*, up to about twenty-six knots by now, so surprised the captain of the gunship that he didn't know whether to fire his cannon or back off.

When *The Sonya* was within a hundred yards of the gunship, I saw a great gush of water from the gunship's stern. The big vessel shuddered in the water and took off to the right. I could hear Vasily laughing all the way from the bridge as he cut across the new wake and plunged onward toward Turkey.

The gunship made another sweeping turn and disappeared. This time, I knew, as it headed back toward *The Sonya*, looming out of the fog, the captain would use his three-incher. He'd blow us out of the water while we were still in Russian territory.

But, as the gunship approached, it began another turn to starboard to come up alongside. The gunship kept up a rapid speed as it began to whiz past us.

I saw sailors along the gunwales raise their rifles, and then I knew the Soviets' plan.

"Hit the deck," I yelled to Tania and Nadia. "They're going to open fire on us."

But we could have stood and watched. The sailors, under their shrewd captain's orders, weren't even aiming at the cabin.

A virtual crescendo of gunfire burst out as the gunship moved past. I heard each individual shot, heard glass shattering and tinkling all over the deck outside.

The gunship went on past, leaving a tremendous wake. *The Sonya*, still churning along at full speed, began to veer off course from the heavy waves left by the gunship.

And I knew.

"They've killed Vasily," I said, getting up. "That was their plan if he didn't stop." I picked up the rifle I'd brought down with me. "You two stay here with Mark," I said. "We're only a few minutes from Turkish waters, but someone has to steer this damned thing or we'll soon be going in circles."

"You're going up to the bridge?" Tania asked. "But the ship will just come by again and shoot you."

"Probably," I said. "But I have to give it a try."

"No, don't," Nadia shouted. "You will die if you go up there. There must be no more killing." Her screams finally turned to unabashed sobbing.

I went topside just as the gunship was making another wide sweep to make another pass at *The Sonya*. I grabbed the wheel, checked the compass, saw that we were several degrees off course. I turned the wheel to starboard and held her there until the compass swung around to a hundred and ninety four.

Turkish waters just ahead. Trabzon three hours beyond that.

I checked the throttle and saw that Vasily had rammed it all the way forward. He lay now in a pool of his own blood against the starboard wall of the wheelhouse. He looked peaceful, beyond fear. I felt a moment's pang for his death, then realized that I might very well follow him in the next few minutes.

The gunship had made its turn and was heading back.

Well, I thought, I won't set myself up as a target the way Vasily had. I turned the wheel hard right and headed directly toward the oncoming gunship. I kept the course, playing "chicken" with the Soviet captain, determined not to turn until he did.

Fortunately, he made his turn to the north. I whipped the wheel to port and shot off southward, hoping against hope that, by the time the gunship got turned around, we would be in Turkish waters.

A thought hit me. The Soviets wouldn't really care about the invisible line that divided the two countries. With no Turkish ships or planes in the area, they could disable us where they chose, then tow us back into Soviet waters.

I snapped on Vasily's radio, picked up the microphone and began announcing: "Mayday, mayday, mayday."

A voice came back in English, thick with Turkish accent.

"We hear you, mayday. Please identify and give position."

I gave him more than that. After identifying *The Sonya* and giving our position as best I could, I told the guy on the radio that we were being pursued by a Soviet gunship that was already in Turkish waters. I was fudging a bit on that, but it would soon turn out to be true. And I was desperate.

"Hold your course," the Turkish-accented voice said in English. "No matter what happens, hold your course."

He switched off and I felt very alone in that wheelhouse with the dead captain and the shattered windows and windscreen. I wasn't alone long. The Soviet gunship was maneuvering for another pass, to kill the man at the helm. Me.

I kept the fishing boat on course, but watched as the gunship approached from behind on the port side. When its bow was alongside me, I began to move the wheel just slightly to port, narrowing the gap between the two vessels. The captain didn't seem to notice. His eyes were on the sailors who had reloaded and were ready for another barrage.

When I saw the sailors raise their rifles, I slipped the lockstrap over the helm and hit the deck like a bag of wet sand. The chattering of automatic weapons started up with a frenzy, filling the wheelhouse with ricocheting, splattering, thundering copper-sheathed bullets.

But the barrage abruptly stopped. I heard whistles and horns and shouts over there on the gunship. The sailors themselves had raised the hue and cry when they saw that the two ships were about to collide. *The Sonya*, riding hard on the new course I'd set, was only inches away from the side of the gunship.

With a throbbing rush of power, the gunship heeled to port again, bobbling us in her wake. I leaped from the floor, unhooked the lockstrap, set *The Sonya* back on one ninety-four, and watched the big gunship make another wide turn.

This time, I was certain, the captain wouldn't depend on sailors and small weapons to eliminate the man on the bridge. This time, I knew in my guts, he'd use the three-inch cannon. He'd blow both the man and the bridge to bits.

The gunship was just touching our wake again when I heard voices on the radio. Russian voices. Muscovite Russian. I caught the gist of the order. The gunship was being ordered to stand down, to stop. We were almost in Turkish waters.

The exultant feeling in my throat soon died. I saw why the

gunship had been ordered to stand down. Six Soviet helicopters, sailing at about a thousand feet, were making a beeline toward the fleeing *Sonya*.

The Russians obviously had heard my "mayday" call and had decided it wouldn't be wise for the gunship to be in Turkish waters. But the helicopters, with weapons just as powerful as the gunship's, would make fast work of us from a distance. Or, if they did cross the line, they'd be able to flit back so fast it would make your head swim.

It was over.

But I kept the boat running full out, over or not. I began to zigzag, just to make the Soviet gunners have to work for their day's pay. And I kept waiting for one of those two-two whizzers to erupt from the nose of one of the helicopter gunships.

When nothing happened, I scanned the skies ahead.

And there they came. Three Turkish and three American helicopters, each bearing the NATO emblem, came churning over the water from the south.

Just when I was ready to rejoice that we'd won and that the Soviet choppers would back off, a strange but hardly unpredictable thing happened.

The opposing helicopters began to swing back and forth, like a dozen boxers in a ring, six boxers to a team, each waiting for the other to swing first.

It was a standoff. The radio crackled in English.

"Chopper One to *Sonya*," the voice said. "Strongly advise that you cut all engines."

When the chopper pilot clicked off, I heard a disturbing roar from above. Jet fighters were streaking up from the south. Good, that gave us the advantage. And then a roar came from behind and I saw three MiG 23 fighters coming in from the north.

Still a standoff. Maybe we had won, maybe we hadn't. One touchy trigger finger up there not only would destroy *The Sonya* and us along with it, that finger could start up the kind of fighting that the whole world wants to avoid.

I cut the engines, as ordered, and watched the planes and helicopters jockey for position on either side of the international line. All the helicopters came down low, and one

Soviet chopper even got so close that I could see the pilot grinning at me, grinning like death.

And then the least expected event occurred.

The cabin door burst open and Mark Koselke, looking like a wild man, dashed out onto the deck. He had his .30 caliber rifle in his hands. I saw Tania try to pull him back inside, but he fended her off and took dead aim on the helicopter that hovered just over the stern of *The Sonya*.

My God, if he fired that rifle, all hell would break loose. Even if he missed, the Soviet pilots would all open fire. And, if that happened, the Americans and Turks would join in.

One rifle shot from a half-drugged, revenge-crazed former American Army Intelligence captain could very well be the first shot of World War Three.

I was just raising Wilhelmina to shoot Mark Koselke in the head, figuring it would be the only way to stop him, when I saw a blur from the cabin door.

From that blur came a piercing cry, "No more killing!"

It was Nadia. She struck Mark Koselke broadside and knocked him against the railing. His rifle went sailing into the ocean.

And that simple action, that child's cry for peace, for no more killing, seemed to touch the minds and the hearts of all those pilots flying around above us.

In two minutes, the Soviet planes and helicopters were rumbling off to the north. The American and Turkish jets made one last cut across our bow and then streaked off south. The helicopters began to peel off and head south, one by one. All except Chopper One.

"This is Chopper One," the now familiar voice said. "Start engines. See you in Trabzon."

NINETEEN

"Mr. Parson, your table for four is ready."

I nodded thanks to Melvin, the best headwaiter in the finest seafood restaurant in Washington, and led Tania into the dining room. Behind us, Mark walked with a short, tentative step. On his arm, animated and exuberant and smiling wildly at everything and everyone, Nadia Koselkovitch marched with a quick, happy beat.

We were seated at a rear window overlooking the Washington Channel and East Potomac Park. Lights on the slowly cruising boats looked like low stars on the clear July night.

"May I have Oysters Rockefeller?" Nadia asked when we were seated. "A man I talked to on the plane from London said I shouldn't miss a chance to have them."

I smiled at the sweet-faced girl, patted her hand. "Tonight, lovely Nadia," I said, "you may have anything you wish."

We were celebrating. Thanks to David Hawk's help, Mark and Tania Koselke had been cleared of all charges on the passport business. And the Soviet Embassy was making no noise at all about the killings of a dozen-plus commissars in the Kharkov-Rostov region. And Nadia, to her immense delight, was going to summer school preparatory to entering high school as a freshman in the autumn.

As for me, I'd received the usual chewing out by David Hawk for nearly causing an international crisis, for not re-

173

solving the problem in hours instead of days, for general principles. And then I'd gotten a rare compliment. A left-handed one, but a compliment.

"If it hadn't been for your damn-fool attempt to ram that Soviet gunship when it came alongside that last time," Hawk had said, "you'd all be fishbait by now. I suppose it was a good ploy."

I didn't tell him that I'd learned the ploy from a master, from poor old Vasily Merkolov who was now resting in a Turkish grave. Compliments from Hawk are too rare to be watered down by humility.

For the time being, Mark was unemployed. The Army wouldn't take him back. But he had decided against going back to Russia to finish off the two or three commissars he hadn't been able to knock off. He and Tania were staying home, taking care of Nadia. And their father, though saddened by Mark's crazy antics, cherished young Nadia as though she were the last Koselkovitch left on earth, which, of course, she might have been.

"Oh, I love them," Nadia said when she had dived into her Oysters Rockefeller. "Why do they call them that?"

"Didn't you look at the price on the menu?" Mark said, grinning.

Nadia smiled. "Mr. Parson told me not to look at the prices. Really, why do they call them Oysters Rockefeller?"

I was just starting to give her the answer, when I felt a presence at my left elbow, then one at my right. I looked to my left and there was big ugly Mikhail, the garlic-oozing goon from the Soviet Embassy. To my right was Ivan Zygorsky, the handsome blond man who was first deputy at the embassy. I leaned back in my chair and smiled at Zygorsky.

"Sorry we don't have a bigger table," I said with a zing of sarcasm. "Even if we did, I doubt that we'd ask you to join us."

Zygorsky smiled. He was genuinely pleased with my honesty.

"We have just finished," he said, "Mikhail and I. I heard your name called, and had to see you for a moment."

I looked around the table. Mark's face had gone grim, even

angry. Tania watched the men with thinly disguised dislike. Nadia gaped at the Soviets, then shuddered as though in fear. She suddenly lost interest in her oysters.

"Okay," I said. "You've seen me. Now, how about letting us enjoy our meal?"

"Surely," Zygorsky said. "I am just curious about a recent matter near the town of Makeevka in the Ukraine. Would you or your new friends happen to know anything about it?"

"What event is that?" I really didn't want to know, but I wanted the man to speak his piece and get the hell out.

"It would seem that someone else has taken up where this Nick Carter fellow left off," Zygorsky said. "Two weeks ago, Commissar Vladimir Kulinin was killed by a shotgun blast not far from the village of Makeevka. Last week, Commissar Ivan Dushkin was killed in a similar way in his dacha south of Rostov."

I shrugged, working like the dickens to keep from breaking out in a broad smile, or into laughter.

"Can't help you, Ivan," I said. "As you and your people must know, we've all been undergoing debriefing and all manner of things since early June. If you'd like to check. . ."

"I have checked," he said. "None of you here was directly involved, but I thought perhaps you could shed some light."

"Sorry. I don't have the foggiest idea of who else would want to knock off crooked commissars. Do you?"

He blushed pinkly, muttered something unintelligible and walked away. Mikhail gave us all a last withering look and followed his boss outside.

When they were gone, I could contain the laughter no longer. Mark, Tania and Nadia looked at me with quizzical looks on their faces.

"What is it? What's so funny?" Tania said.

I couldn't tell them about Sergei Yaslov and his shotgun, or his sons and their rifles. I couldn't tell them that old Sergei was getting even for what had happened to his good friend Vasily Merkolov. But I could tell them one thing.

"I think," I said, winking at Nadia and Tania and then

staring into Mark Koselke's serious eyes, "that you might have started something. I think you've given some people ideas, people who are fed up with being pushed around."

"You mean a Russian killed those commissars?" Mark asked.

"Beats me," I lied. "But keep your ears open. I don't think we've heard the last of the killing of the commissars."

DON'T MISS THE NEXT NEW
NICK CARTER SPY THRILLER

THE YUKON TARGET

"He didn't clear me as I thought he would, Nick," Laraine Shadwell explained. "I can't get to the duty roster and find out what posts are being patrolled. There are at least three possibles that take in that portion of the camp."

I studied the crude map scratched in the dust on the floor of the *barubaras*. From all that Laraine had said, my job of getting into the files for this camp had become significantly more dangerous. The possibility of discovery heightened, I had to be even more alert. With the gung-ho survivalist types running around loose, even that might not be enough.

"Can you create some sort of diversion if it looks as if they'll find me?" I asked. Laraine shook her head. I couldn't figure out if she meant that she couldn't or wouldn't.

Looking out the door into the increasingly cold night, I saw nothing. The sun had set almost an hour earlier. With the tall, craggy peaks surrounding the camp, night came suddenly and absolutely once the sun dipped out of sight. I slid through the door and quietly closed it behind me. The frigid bite of the evening worked at my hands and exposed face. I ignored it as I moved away, picking my path carefully.

To go directly to the files center might be my best bet, yet something told me to be more circumspect. Chapman was paranoid. He wouldn't let just anyone walk straight in. No matter what Laraine said or had been told, there were quite a few sophisticated electronics gadgets scattered around the camp. Someone somewhere monitored them and I didn't know where. Nor did I really want to find out. Better to avoid those electronic snoopers altogether.

The crunch of boots on gravel sent me scurrying for cover. I dived behind a dark lump of rock and waited. Less than a minute later I saw a guard rubbing hands together for warmth and stamping his feet. Slung over his shoulder was a high-powered rifle. For a fleeting instant I thought of the guard I'd killed up in the hills. Was this man another frightened auto worker out of a job and looking for a way of surviving in a world he barely understood? Was he another Chapman dupe? Or was he one of the cadre, one of the rulers of this well-armed giggling academy?

He had the rifle pulled off his shoulder and was fumbling to get his finger onto the trigger by the time I vaulted the rock and swung a haymaker directly for his face.

He slipped on an icy patch and went down heavily, the rifle falling from his grip. I kicked it back in the direction from which I'd come. Then Hugo slid from his sheath.

"No!" the man gasped, seeing death approaching.

I didn't let him get out a second word. My life depended on his permanent silence. Hot geysers of steam rose as my stiletto sank into the hollow just under his chin. I watched as his hot blood cooled swiftly in the air and produced that grisly vapor.

I waited a few minutes then slid forward and onto the path to continue toward the hut containing the files. I found myself more attuned to watching where I walked, how I moved, what happened around me. And that saved me. One of the electronic traps would have snared me if I hadn't become as cautious as a mouse in a cat factory.

The detector was perfectly suited for this climate. Tiny, barely larger than a lead pencil, the infrared detector guarded the path. The more the temperature dropped, the more sensitive the IR device became to human body heat. I studied it from a few feet away, peering at it until I decided how best to disable it. Approaching it was out of the question; that would trigger an alarm.

Probing the ground nearby uncovered the lead-in wires. I spent the next ten minutes scrapping off insulation and working out the best way of shorting out one wire against the other. When I'd finished, the device was out of commission. Unless a human had been specifically watching the readout when I touched one wire to the other and noticed a current surge, I was in free.

I went directly to the door of the sod house containing all of Chapman's files. A quick check showed no alarms on the door. I went in and looked around. One small kerosene lamp had been left burning. Whether this meant someone would return soon or not was beyond my powers of deduction. Getting the information I wanted and getting the hell out was my best protection now.

Chapman kept impeccable records. I had no trouble at all finding the duty rosters, the training records, the lists of graduates and future hopefuls for this polar training course. A small camera photographed the records in the dim light.

I finished the last page and closed the file drawer when I felt an odd constriction in my chest. Something was very wrong. I glanced around and saw nothing, but the feeling persisted. The faint whine of wind through tiny crevices around the wooden door was the only sound in the sod house. And something was very, very wrong.

Pressing an ear against the door accomplished nothing except giving me a mild case of frostbite. I started to open the door, then saw it. The alarm was so tiny it would have required a full crew to spot it normally. When I'd entered, a partially frozen wire had pulled the device out of the sod where it had been hidden.

I'd triggered a silent alarm when I entered.

My mind went into overdrive. I'd been in here long enough for the entire camp to be mobilized and waiting for me to emerge through that door. I went back to the file cabinets and frantically searched for something to give me an edge. A bottom drawer filled with odds and ends also gave me the best present possible: Wilhelmina. Seizing my Luger, I checked and made sure it was loaded. Spare clips of 9mm ammo were in the drawer, too. I took them and continued looking.

Nothing else of interest surfaced. Racing for the back of the sod house, all too conscious of the time element weighing more and more heavily, I began digging through the heavy dirt walls. Like a gopher I burrowed and soon felt the crisp, cold air against my face. A hole just about large enough for my body yawned when the door to the *barabaras* smashed inward.

Chapman's voice was shrill and unmistakable.

"Kill the son of a bitch! Kill him!"

Heavy bullets smashed into the dirt walls all around me.

—From *THE YUKON TARGET*
A New Nick Carter Spy Thriller
From Charter in July

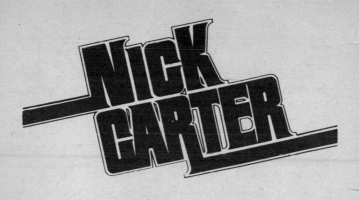

☐ 05381-5	**BEIRUT INCIDENT**	$2.25	
☐ 14172-2	**THE DEATH STAR AFFAIR**		$2.50
☐ 14169-2	**DEATHLIGHT**	$2.50	
☐ 15244-9	**THE DOMINICAN AFFAIR**		$2.50
☐ 17014-5	**THE DUBROVNIK MASSACRE**		$2.25
☐ 18124-4	**EARTH SHAKER**	$2.50	
☐*63176-3	**THE PARISIAN AFFAIR**		$2.50
☐ 65858-X	**THE PEMEX CHART**	$1.95	
☐*67081-4	**PLEASURE ISLAND**		$2.50
☐ 71133-2	**THE REDOLMO AFFAIR**	$1.95	

Available at your local bookstore or return this form to:

 CHARTER BOOKS
Book Mailing Service
P.O. Box 690, Rockville Centre, NY 11571

Please send me the titles checked above. I enclose _____.
Include $1.00 for postage and handling if one book is ordered; 50¢ per book for
two or more. California, Illinois, New York and Tennessee residents please add
sales tax.

NAME _____

ADDRESS _____

CITY _____ STATE/ZIP _____

(allow six weeks for delivery)   A8

Bestselling Books

- ☐ 80701-1 **TICKETS** Richard Brickner $3.25
- ☐ 21888-1 **EXPANDED UNIVERSE** Robert A. Heinlein $3.50
- ☐ 38288-6 **JANISSARIES** J.E. Pournelle $2.75
- ☐ 23189-6 **FEDERATION** H. Beam Piper $2.95
- ☐ 47807-7 **THE LEFT HAND OF DARKNESS** Ursula K. LeGuin $2.50
- ☐ 48518-9 **LIVE LONGER NOW** Jon N. Leonard, J.L. Hofer & N. Pritikin $2.95
- ☐ 48522-7 **LIVE LONGER NOW COOKBOOK** Jon N. Leonard & Elaine A. Taylor $2.95
- ☐ 21772-9 **CASCA: THE ETERNAL MERCENARY** Barry Sadler $2.50
- ☐ 80581-7 **THIEVES' WORLD** Robert Lynn Asprin, Ed. $2.95
- ☐ 34232-9 **THE HOLLOW MEN** Sean Flannery $3.50
- ☐ 83288-1 **TWILIGHT'S BURNING** Diane Guest $3.25